THE RIVERHOUSE STORIES

How Pubah S. Queen
and Lazy LaRue
Save the World

The Riverhouse Stories

How
Pubah S. Queen
and Lazy LaRue
Save the
World

By Andrea Carlisle

Illustrated by
Mary Narkiewicz

Cover art by
Debi Berrow

CALYX BOOKS
Corvallis, Oregon

Portions of
this book originally
appeared in *Calyx, A Journal
of Art and Literature by Women*
Funding for this book was provided
in part by a grant from the
Oregon Arts Commission

Book and cover
design by Debi Berrow
Book illustrations by Mary Narkiewicz
Original cover art by Debi Berrow

Published by CALYX BOOKS
P.O. BOX B, CORVALLIS
OREGON 97339

Library of Congress
Cataloging-in-Publication Data:
Carlisle, Andrea, 1944-
The riverhouse stories.
I. Title.
PS3553.A717R5 1986 813'.54 86-20783
ISBN 0-934971-01-3 (pbk.)

Epigraph reprinted
from *United States*
©1984 by Laurie Anderson
with permission of the author

Printed in the United States of America

Any resemblance
to persons living or dead
is purely whimsical

This book is printed on acid free paper

For Sandra . . . in celebration

Foreword

These are stories not to be skimmed, but savored, memorable not just for what they tell, but how they tell it. They are not quite like any other stories I, or you, most likely, have ever read.

I remember the first time I heard some of these tales, at Hightower, when they were not *The Riverhouse Stories* at all, but a birthday present from Andrea for Sandra. I remember a tea-and-cookies conversation between Andrea and my daughter, then three, about why *shouldn't* any two people who love each other a lot and like to live together be allowed to get married, and how a new piece called "Whether Or Not to Marry" magically appeared in the manuscript a few weeks later. I remember the rainy spring afternoon Andrea and I spent on our knees in my then-office, with stories spread out all around us, trying to discern just the right order to put them in to turn them from a birthday present into a real book.

I remember, too, a conversation with the New York editor to whom we sent them.

"You're right," she said. "They're quite wonderful. It's too bad we can't publish them."

"Why not?" I asked.

"Who would read them?"

"Well, just about everybody," I said.

"That's just it," the editor told me. "There is no publishing category called 'Everybody.' There's women's literature and there's children's literature and there's real literature, and there's fantasy, and there's humor and romance and adventure and inspiration and well, you know. Please tell Andrea Carlisle she's a very good writer and that if she ever writes anything normal, I'd be delighted to see it."

The editor was right, as far as she went. Andrea *is* a fine writer and *The Riverhouse Stories* do defy the easy labels publishers are so fond of putting on their books. They have something in common with all the aforementioned categories, and fit neatly in none. That is, of course, what makes them so delightful.

These stories have the tart sweetness of wild blackberries. They are charming, as old houses and genuine eccentrics are. They are funny, wise, yet with nothing of the know-it-all about them. They are deeply worldly but have no traffic with despair, tenaciously advancing the notion that the earth *can* be made better by living gently and joyously upon it.

The Riverhouse Stories are firmly rooted in the physical place called Oregon and the universal human space called love. They are brave and quirky and, even on a dozenth reading, remarkably fresh. Now, at last, through the vision and commitment of CALYX BOOKS, they are about to find their rightful audience.

Which is, as Pubah herself says, Everyone!

Joyce Thompson
2 August 1986

Acknowledgments

The Riverhouse Stories would not exist as a book without the encouragement and vision of Margarita Donnelly. With Margarita's support, along with Lisa Domitrovich and other friends at *Calyx*, these little tales have found a context in which to live. Thanks to an award from the Oregon Arts Commission, I have had some time given to me to finish this book.

For her commitment to my writing and for her friendship, I am deeply grateful to Rachel MacMaster Lowrie, and to James and Rolfe N. Lowrie who, along with Rachel, have given me their intelligent guidance over the years. Thanks to Alexandra Thompson-Steele whose questions inspire whole stories for answers.

Special thanks to my brother, Michael, for being my first teacher in the domains of friendship and loyalty. I am indebted to him, to my parents, and to Mattie Hamery for the wit, imagination and delight in storytelling they have shared with me all my life.

The spirit that has guided this book is a community spirit. For their confidence, their good humor and their wisdom, I undoubtedly owe my very life to friends in Portland, Seattle and San Francisco.

Some people read these stories with special attention as the manuscript took shape. I would like to thank them for their enthusiasm and ideas: Joyce Thompson, Tom and Marva Belden, Mary Narkiewicz, Linda Gioja, Salli Archibald and Jerene Kirkman. Bill Masciarelli's inspired contribution to this work, and to my life, has been invaluable.

I am grateful to Jodie Slattery not only for the poems she gave to this book, but for the intelligence and delight she brings to all of us who are fortunate enough to call her a friend.

My love and gratitude to other friends and influences: Claudia Johnson, Susan Walsh, Mark Alter, Patrick and Sharon Slattery, Geoffrey Gioja, the Cahn family, the Turner family, the Archibald family, the Larsen family and the Doughton family; Jean Johnson, Kathryn Hunt, Werner Erhard, Ramakrishna, and Van Morrison.

Andrea Carlisle
July 1986

". . . and so you're born and so they say,
'You're free,' so happy birthday."

Laurie Anderson, From *United States*

PART I: *THE RIVER*

The Riverhouse
◆ ◆ ◆

Pubah and Lazy LaRue moved to a riverhouse in the winter. That house just sat right on the water, with some logs under it and some big blank spots under it too so that it tipped over to one side. When the snow came down heavy, the whole house almost sank. Fortunately, it did not snow too often in Oregon. This house had holes in it and not much heat and, snow or not, the winter was very, very cold.

Pubah kept saying to Lazy LaRue (who was always shivering), "Don't you worry. We'll fix this place right up."

She said she would bring home things to do that with. She brought home a thing called a "service." She said it was for the electricity and that her boss electrician had given it to her. Pubah was learning how to be an electrician and she knew all about the box. It was a big rectangular blue panel with switches inside. She propped it up against the refrigerator and said, "This is very expensive. I got it for free." She smiled.

They didn't have any wood to burn in the woodstove so Pubah lassoed a log right out of the river and they cut it up and burned it. "Don't you worry," Pubah said, as Lazy LaRue sat by the fire. "I'm going to fix this place up so good."

One day she brought home a big round wooden barrel, stuffed it full of kindling, and put it on the deck.

"There!" she cried.

She brought home little boxes of red and yellow plastic nipples and said they were for the electricity too. Pubah loved electricity things.

She brought home copper wrapped in black tubing. "To sell," she explained. She brought home clear plastic boxes of screws and long strings of nails hooked together on plastic tape. "For building with." She brought 120 planks of 1x6's for the bedroom ceiling and nailed up a few. "Nice?" she asked, nodding in response to her own question.

She brought metal coverings for lightswitches that she found somewhere. "Just like the hospitals have!" she sang out joyfully, holding them up over the lightswitch holes she had gouged out one day when she had begun to rewire the house. She tore down walls and together they demolished a huge fireplace that was making the houseboat tip over. Pubah began to strip wallpaper, began to build a toolchest where the

1

fireplace had been, began to do sheetrocking, began to nail up some wood in the bathroom, began to pull planks from the side of the house so she could see under it, and began to get tired.

They bought a canoe. Pubah knocked part of the deck out so they could get in and out of their canoe easily. They got in often. "I love this!" Pubah would scream.

When summer came, Lazy LaRue stopped shivering so much and began to love the riverhouse too. They had good neighbors and enough to eat and they couldn't have been happier.

Baby Ducks
◆ ◆ ◆

In the summer all the people along the riverhouse moorage talked about baby ducks. "Seen any?" they asked each other as they passed on the walkway going to work.

"Nope, not yet." They shook their heads until, finally, one day one of them would say, "Canoed out yesterday and saw some eggs on Duck Island."

This announcement was passed up and down through all the riverhouses.

Duck Island was a long grassy float covered with wild bushes and ferns. No one could remember how it came to be in front of the house Pubah and Lazy lived in. It was attached to two long poles driven in by the waterlord years before, and it was a perfect haven for the half-wild ducks to sleep on and keep their eggs a safe distance from dogs and cats. The ducks came quacking for food every night at dinnertime.

When baby ducks appeared, these same Oregonians who could wield chainsaws as easily as toothbrushes, these masters of the 4-wheel drive, would show up on their decks and cause themselves to sound exactly like ducks. "Quack!" they shouted to the island.

"Quack! Quack!" the mother duck would answer.

"Quack!" the riverhouse people would repeat until the mother duck came over to one of them with her babies following, puffs of brown and gold light on the green surface of the water. Their tiny orange feet fluttered rapidly.

At the deck the mother proudly waited while the humans served her babies bits of bread. The ducklings crawled over logs trying to get the crumbs and toppled head first into the water time and again.

Now and then they would cross the river to visit a moored fisherman who might give them some variety in their diet. The houseboat people waited for them to come back, watching as the mother marshalled them again toward Duck Island, while the downstream current tried to sweep their fluffy bodies toward the ocean. The mother, firm, barked commands to stay in formation: Move those little flappers! Faster! Faster!

Everybody relaxed again when they came fitfully into home waters, narrowly missed by speedboats and waterskiers, their tired bodies bobbing up and down on giant wakes while their mother, serene goddess of

3

the river, demonstrated the head up, neck straight, flat-belly technique that would keep them afloat until they could, at last, bow their heads forward, raise their tiny feet, and step once more onto the safe terrain of Duck Island.

move those flappers

Turning the Riverhouse
◆ ◆ ◆

After several months of life in the riverhouse, Pubah and Lazy noticed that it was facing in the wrong direction. "Hey!" Lazy said one day with mild alarm, "Shouldn't we be facing the river when we look out our front window?"

Instead of facing the river, their front window looked directly into their neighbors' family room.

Pubah agreed with Lazy, incredulous that they hadn't noticed this error before. "Silly us," she said. "Well, we'll just have to turn this riverhouse around."

Lazy went outside and examined the heavy chains holding the thirty-foot riverhouse to the walkway. She thought about the tonnage of logs under the house. Then she looked at their canoe and their supply of lightweight ropes. She came back inside to find Pubah covered with a quilt, reading Einstein.

"We can't do that, Pubah," she said.

"Oh sure we can," Pubah told her.

"How?"

Pubah thought. Then she said, "We'll ask somebody."

They attended a meeting where all the people who lived on the moorage got together and talked about various problems they were having. "Well, we have a problem," Pubah told them. "Our house faces the wrong direction."

"We thought you'd never notice," one of them said. Everybody laughed good-naturedly.

"Don't you worry," a red-haired man named Charlie told her. "We'll be over there tomorrow and turn that baby around."

As they left the meeting Pubah whispered, "See, Lazy? They're going to turn that baby around."

Lazy didn't even try to imagine how they would do it. She went to the store in the morning and bought lots of chips and cheese and crackers and beer. Then they waited.

Plenty of neighbors came. They arrived in motorboats and on foot. They brought long hooked poles and ropes as big around as telephone poles. "This'll be easy," their neighbor Dugan told them. His wife, Sal, stood next to him and nodded. "Easier than you think," she assured them.

5

The neighbors tied the ropes to the corner of the riverhouse and then to the motorboats. They unhooked the chains holding the house to the walkway and then shouted, "Ho!"

The motorboat drivers started their motors and moved downriver. Slowly the long house swung out from the walkway.

"Not too far!" Sal called to the motorboats.

They all called to one another, "There! Whoa! Now! Throw that in! Here, give me that! Stop! Easy! Good!"

"Yes, good," Lazy said in a small voice from the walkway. "Real good."

She watched them pull the house around so that the front window faced exactly onto the river. The whole event only took an hour. The neighbors chained the house up again from the back end to the walkway.

"There you go," the neighbors told Pubah and Lazy, who then offered them the beer and chips and cheese and crackers. Lazy wished she could give them flowers and lobster and the finest wines.

The small boats motored up to the walkway and the people in them drank the beer and smiled. "Like that better?"

Lazy and Pubah rushed inside. Now they could not only see the river, but the tree-lined shore opposite the riverhouses and the bridge in the distance and downriver as well. They invited the neighbors to come inside. Dugan and Sal and Charlie and the others stepped in and looked admiringly out at the water.

"That's better," they said quietly and nodded, then slowly wandered back to their own houses, beer in hand.

Pubah and Lazy spoke with adoration of them the rest of the day and the next and the one after that.

"I like riverlife," Lazy admitted for the first time out loud. "The best thing about it is the people."

Sal and Dugan
◆ ◆ ◆

To Pubah and Lazy, Sal and Dugan were two of the most interesting of all neighbors. Dugan was an anthropologist and Sal was an artist. Sal had set about rebuilding their houseboat from the floor up. She tore things apart and put them back together again in a way that spoke highly of her interior self, to Pubah and Lazy's way of thinking.

Sal came down the walkway from time to time for a visit. Tall, thin, with silver hair and a crooked walking stick, she draped herself in a Mexican cape that had an eagle embroidered in gold threads across its front. She knocked on their door by saying, "Knock, knock."

When Lazy's first story was published Sal brought her the small white stone head of a pharaoh. "Found it in Egypt," she said. "Three or four thousand years old. Keep it in a dry place."

For their birthdays she made them a stained glass window to go in their front door. The window was a brilliant burst of shapes with a sand dollar as part of the design. Above their table she placed a stained glass lamp with signs of the zodiac etched into it and blue beads around the top that came from Venice and China.

"Merry Christmas," she said.

In the summer she canoed by with her daughter swimming behind. This child dressed like a rock star even to swim in the river. The little girl's brother attended his mother and sister from his kayak a short distance away. He was a smart, silent, observant child. "Kayak boy," Pubah and Lazy once said in acknowledgment as he paddled past them. He pretended not to hear.

Dugan liked to tell stories, play the harmonica, and laugh. One night when Lazy and Pubah were on the river in their canoe watching the moon tumble in and out of the black rolling water, they heard a shout. "Whale!" Then a big splash followed by a laugh. "Daddy!"

"Don't call me Daddy! I'm a whale." Dugan was in the water trying to imitate blowhole sounds. Lazy and Pubah canoed over.

"Come on in," he invited.

"I don't go in the water after dark," Lazy told him. "That water's freezing."

"Perfect for whales," Dugan said. "Whales, bananafish and . . ." He grabbed for his little girl on the deck, "whalebabies!" She screamed and giggled into the house.

Dugan came out of the water and he and Sal and Pubah and Lazy sat on the deck for a few hours drinking wine and talking about Mexico and art and houseboat moorages and nearly everything else. They roamed in and out of great pastures of conversation, grazing on death and life, law, magic, and history. The children curled up in blankets on the deck and fell asleep under the stars.

Later, when Lazy and Pubah canoed home again, they were silent. They were filled with the night and with the soft murmurs of voices that had danced out over the river, with the great and small flights of laughter that had taken them up into the night's arms, and with friendship itself which was not so much a thing to have, it seemed, but a way of being. They got out of their canoe, placed the paddles on the deck, came inside the riverhouse, and sat down. For a long time they did not speak, then Lazy looked at Pubah and sighed. "We're just awed by love, I guess."

Pubah nodded. "Awed by love."

Sal

Pubah and the Muskrats
and the River Monster
◆ ◆ ◆

Pubah and Lazy were out on the deck of the riverhouse. Pubah had her pantlegs rolled up and her feet in the cold water.

"Watch out for muskrats," Lazy said casually to her.

"Muskrats?"

"Yes," said Lazy, "there are muskrats in this water. Didn't you know?"

"No!" Pubah said.

"Yep. There are muskrats and they're building nests under the old walkway and they come along every once in a while and see people's toes in the water and think it's the enemy. They just might nibble on your toes."

Pubah pulled her feet out of the water. "I hate things that might be in the water! I hate things that might be in the water!" she cried.

"I know," Lazy said, "I know. But you can put your feet back in the water and move them back and forth really fast. That way you'll scare the muskrats away."

Pubah looked at Lazy and studied her. She didn't know whether or not to trust her, but because it was such a hot day and because she really did

they think its the enemy

9

want her feet in the water, she put them very slowly back in, then quicky moved them back and forth, back and forth, back and forth.

"That's right," Lazy told her. "Not only will you keep the muskrats away, but you'll get lots of exercise."

"You mean like this?" Pubah asked, her legs cutting through the water like pieces of machinery turned on high.

Lazy could hardly tell that they were legs at all. "Exactly," she replied.

"You know," Pubah said, "I'm going to cut this old porch right off this houseboat."

"Oh?"

"See, this porch doesn't work," Pubah pointed out. Lazy saw that the wakes from boats passing by forced the porch up and down so dramatically that the nails were pulled loose and some of the boards were flopping in the breeze.

"This is no longer a real porch," Pubah told her, "but a flexoporch."

"I see," said Lazy.

The next morning Pubah got out on the porch with her Skilsaw.

"Please don't get electrocuted," Lazy begged her.

"Okay," Pubah agreed.

In a little while she called Lazy. "See?"

Sure enough she had cut off all the boards halfway.

Pubah pulled out two chairs and said, "Sit down here with me, Lazy, and let's have a drink of mineral water to celebrate the beginning of our new porch."

They sat in the chairs and began to drink but a boat went by and something happened.

"Whoa!" said Pubah.

"What was that?" Lazy inquired, noticing that whatever it was, it happened right beneath her chair.

Suddenly they heard a terrible rumble, as though a monster who lived under the riverhouse had just been awakened. The monster bounced them right out of their chairs and rolled from under the porch out into the water.

"What in the world is that?" Lazy asked.

It was, in fact, the biggest log either of them had ever seen. It was not a timber and it was not a pole. It was a tree that had been living for many years under their porch.

The log began to drift away. Pubah jumped out onto it and Lazy threw her a rope.

"Tie her up!" Pubah shouted.

"Okay!" Lazy shouted back. She tied the log to the riverhouse. Pubah jumped back onto the porch which was now angled drastically down into the river. When they sat on their chairs again, it seemed that the slightest wave would spill them into the water.

"Well!" Pubah looked with pride at her new log. "That log is really something. Do you know how much we could sell that log for?"

"No," said Lazy.

"Lots," said Pubah.

"Oh," Lazy said.

Pubah grinned and grinned at her new log.

Life was sure interesting with Pubah, Lazy thought. And profitable too.

Elby and the Million Dollars

◆ ◆ ◆

Elby wanted a million dollars.

"I just want about a million dollars," she said sweetly. "Then I would stop worrying about money. Just one million dollars. I know it's silly to want that. I know *everybody* wants that, but I want it too. I want to pay all my bills, give away a lot of presents, buy a new car and stereo, and get some new clothes. I just want a million bucks. Is that too much to ask?"

Pubah and Lazy looked at each other.

"Absolutely not," they said.

They loved their friend, Elby, and wanted her to have whatever her heart desired. Elby was always being useful to other people, so they agreed that one million dollars was probably going to be just the first in a series of installments the universe would give her as acknowledgment.

"Easy peasy," they told her.

Elby started a bug device company. Bugs and rodents were chased out of houses by a small black box that emitted a high-pitched whine only bugs, rodents, dogs, and humans could hear.

"There!" Elby said. "It works. How long do you think it will take for my one million dollars to come?"

"Can't be too long," Pubah told her.

"Nope, coming soon, I betcha," Lazy agreed.

Many, many people bought a bug device. Elby added up the numbers. "Looks good," she assured herself.

One night Elby had a dream that she was sitting on her porch eating olives. The mailman came with an enormous envelope and it had Elby's name and address on it.

"Here you go," he said to her.

Elby thanked him and ripped open the big fat envelope. A million dollars came tumbling out in large bills and quarters.

"Oh joy, joy!" she shouted.

Her boyfriend came rushing out of the house. "What is it?"

"It's my million dollars," Elby rejoiced, "at last!"

"Well, it's about time," he sighed. "I thought it was taking awfully long. Are you happy now?"

"Happy!" she smiled with her big teeth showing and her eyes almost

shut by her grinning. "Happy happy happy happy happy happy!"

She visited the riverhouse the next day and told Pubah and Lazy about the dream.

"Good sign," they told her.

"Well, even if I never do make a million dollars from bug devices, at least I've had all that money once—although I was unconscious at the time."

"That's what I like about our friends," said Lazy, "easily satisfied."

"Ever so easily. Rather a nice quality." Pubah patted Elby on the back. Elby just smiled.

Pubah and the Timekeeping System
◆ ◆ ◆

Pubah was stumped by time.

She had a lot of work to do in the world and tried really hard to get it all done. When she was already working, dressed up like an electrician and crawling around inside enormous pipes with her toolbelt on, even then she thought of all the work she had to do and, often, she would pull out a pencil and write herself a note about it.

She stuffed these notes into her shirt pocket and forgot about them. Lazy found one of the papers one day when Pubah came home. She was hugging her and heard a crinkle so she reached into Pubah's pocket and pulled out the paper. It was all folded up. Lazy unfolded it and read Pubah's note to herself.

"Finish college!" it demanded.

There were so many things to do that every night Pubah went to bed moaning, "There's so much I didn't do!"

She decided to take a class on time from Elby. Elby knew all about time, managed it very well. Elby wore her red shoes and led the class. "I have a system," she told them.

She wrote notes about her system in pretty letters with magic markers on a board and made recommendations. Pubah was very excited and ordered the recommended timekeeping system.

When it arrived she pushed aside all she had to do that day so that she could put the new timekeeping system together. It consisted of a notebook with many pages. Each day was a page and each page was divided into hours and half hours.

"Perfect!" Pubah cried from her usual vast storehouse of excitement.

Lazy watched Pubah put her notebook together and write down in it all that she had to do. When she was all finished, Pubah said, "There!" and slammed the notebook shut.

She carried her timekeeping system everywhere.

"I can keep everything I need to do right in here," she said, holding up the notebook for Lazy to see. "Now it will all get done."

"I see," said Lazy.

Pubah raced around just as fast as ever, but now she paused occasionally to check off something she had accomplished in her timekeeping system checkmark column.

14

Lazy liked it that Pubah was happy and was getting organized. With Pubah on a system, maybe the work that needed to get done on the riverhouse would get listed, prioritized, and checked off. Maybe the living room wall would be completed and the bathroom sink repaired. Maybe there would be a new washing machine hose installed and carpeting put down in the bedrooms. Maybe the front porch would be fixed and new decking put on the sides of the house. Perhaps the bathroom would get painted. Lazy dreamed great dreams. If these things were listed, surely they would get done.

One morning a few days later, Lazy found Pubah looking sad. She was sitting at the table crying over her notebook.

"Nothing's getting done!" insisted Pubah. "I can't do this thing!" Lazy looked at the timekeeping notebook. "There aren't very many checkmarks," Pubah said. "I'm not accomplishing everything."

Lazy saw the problem. She looked at the line between nine and nine-thirty a.m. on Saturday. Pubah had squeezed many things onto the line:

> Tune up car
> Do taxes
> Figure out what to wear to K's party
> Eat something
> Write Granny
> Practice sax
> Call Elby

She carried the timekeeping system with her everywhere.

"Oh, I think I see the problem," Lazy told her. "You're very good at writing things down."

"Yes?" Pubah looked up sweetly through her tears.

"But you have to figure out how long something's going to take. Each thing takes some length of time, you see."

"Some length of time," Pubah said, trying to follow the words. Then, lighting up, she said, "Oh! Each one takes time! You have to figure out how long it will take. I get it. I get it." She smiled. "You're a genius," she said to Lazy, who rolled her eyes.

Pubah picked up her notebook and rushed to a corner to sit down and figure out how long things took.

Why, oh why, did Pubah think she was a genius, Lazy wondered. It worried her. It made her want to rush out and take an intelligence quotient test.

At two a.m. Lazy was awakened from a deep dreamy sleep by the song "In the Gloaming" played on a saxophone only one thin wall away.

"Pubah!" she called out. There was some more song.

"Pubah!" she called louder.

"Not much longer," shouted Pubah through the wall. "I did everything on my list today and all I have left is practicing my saxophone from two until two-thirty. That's how long it takes. I'll come to bed then because I sleep from two-thirty-two until six-thirty-four."

"Good," said Lazy.

"I love you!" shouted Pubah.

"I love you too," Lazy called, slipping into the gloaming.

Creativity
◆ ◆ ◆

L azy wanted to write stories, but there was a problem. She loved being with her friends. The writing of stories required hour upon hour alone in a back corner of the riverhouse with only her pets to keep her company. So devoted were her friends to her work that they did not even call during her writing hours.

Sometimes she just sat and missed humanity. After a long while of doing that she would hear a voice, a familiar voice, her mother's voice, in fact. It said, quietly at first, then progressively louder, "Well, this won't buy the baby a shirt." Since Lazy was a child she had known what that expression meant. It meant, let's get to work.

Sometimes Lazy then got to work. Sometimes she didn't. Sometimes the loneliness was like an elephant sitting on her chest and she couldn't move. The stacks of blank paper on her desk remained untouched and the black shroud covered the typewriter all day while Lazy spent her time thinking, "Is writing the right thing for me to be doing with my life? Why can't I be out there with everybody else?" These questions led nowhere.

Lazy put photographs of her friends, her parents, her grandparents, and other writers all around her room. "That's helpful," she decided.

When she was actually writing, there was nothing and no one to be missing. There was only her own voice, unmysterious, welcome, certain. Pictures passed from her mind into language while she watched the transformation on the edge of disbelief.

At parties and other gatherings many people queried Lazy about writing. They had all kinds of questions, but how could she answer them? Really, what they were saying was that they wanted to write too.

"Did you ever think of writing a story about my grandparents coming over here from Russia in 1909?" they might say.

Or, "I once snuck past the red zone on Mt. St. Helens. Did I ever tell you about that? Boy, that'd be something to write."

Or, "I've always wanted to write about the time my kid and her friend took a bunch of dixie cups up to her room, see, and spread them all over the place? And then you know what they did? They peed in every single one of them . . . ."

"Write that," Lazy told them.

They said, "Can't." Or, "Someday maybe." Or, "Haw." Or, "Well, I'm

Lazy at her desk

no writer." Or, "It'd never sell."

"Write it anyway," she urged them.

"Naw."

At these events she sometimes felt like a doctor who was approached for free consulting and whose recommendations were not to be followed.

Gently, she added, "It's hard when you think about it, but after you write for a while, and you begin to hear your own voice, it's worth it."

Sometimes, back in her room, even with the photographs around her, Lazy thought that her loneliness was bigger than her love for her own voice and the writing. At those times, she had to switch it around and include the loneliness in her day, rather than have the day be all loneliness and not any writing. This didn't take strength so much as remembering that she could do that.

When she could remember, she got to watch the words tumble across the page again. She followed their fast tracks like a hunting dog sniffing out game, only the game was all in the following and the listening, the rush of the pen across the page making symbols. She knew then, without thinking about it, that all the forces in the world caused the pen to move —all her friends and those who were not her friends, all that had happened and not happened in her life, all that was and was not. The faces in the room looked on silently—Flannery O'Connor and Eudora Welty, Grandfather Emerson, Willa Cather, her friends Elby, Kalin, Suzana, Catlin and Al, as well as Colette, Aunt Meta, Dolly Parton, Pubah, of course, and others. This whole crowd of friends in the room and the outside world and eternity inspired her. Every time she finished a piece of work, the same thought occurred to her: The only thing that could equal the writing would be giving what she wrote back to them.

The History of the Riverhouse
◆ ◆ ◆

W hen the old woman came, Lazy was feeding the ducks.
"Yo!" the woman shouted from the walkway, and when
Lazy turned around she saw her, plump and extravagantly
cosmeticized, with hair in pink curlers protected by a filmy
blue scarf.

"Can I come aboard?"

"Of course." Lazy motioned for her to step onto the deck.

"My, my, my, my," the woman was saying as she held her purse tightly
and climbed over a big log onto the deck. "My, my, my."

"Nancy Stillwater," she said, holding out her hand.

"Lazy MacIntosh," Lazy introduced herself. They pumped each other's
hands energetically.

"My," Nancy Stillwater said again, peeking through the open top of
the Dutch door. "I used to live here," she whispered confidentially.

"You don't say!"

"May I come in?"

"Sure." Lazy opened the door and they went inside. The woman shook
her head and looked around.

"When did you live here?" Lazy asked.

"Well, my husband built me this place in the thirties. I wanted to live
on the river. Took a fancy to it." She pushed her sunglasses up onto the
bridge of her nose and smiled. "Liked the ducks, you know. Say, where's
the fireplace?"

"Oh we had to take that out. You see, the houseboat was tipping over
because the bricks weighed so much and there was an awful roaring wind
that came sailing down into it. . . ."

"Oh, that's a shame," Nancy Stillwater interrupted. "I liked that
fireplace. Yes. I liked it very much. Used to have one upstairs too."

"Upstairs?" There was now no upstairs.

"Yes," the woman said, with her face close up to Lazy's. "This was
originally a two-story house until the Columbus Day storm. Why, that
day there was a fire goin' here in the fireplace and the whole top floor just
blew off. Whoosh!" Nancy Stillwater waved her hand and eliminated the
already invisible top floor of the riverhouse.

"With the fire still going?" Lazy glanced at her woodstove.

"Yes indeedy, young lady. That fire just kept on burning. Miracle the place didn't burn down, wouldn't you say?"

Lazy shivered. "Indeedy."

"So you took that out. Tsk." She made shame sounds. "Tsk, tsk."

"Yeah." Lazy looked at the clean sweep of wall where the fireplace had been. Pubah had put some of her own paintings on it. "Yeah," she said again, "replaced it with sheetrock. Sheetrock and art."

Nancy was willing to tell all. "This house, you know, has quite the history."

"I guess so."

"This very house," Nancy said as she looked around, "was once swept away by a flood."

Lazy began to wish she didn't know, as soon as she knew, that houseboats got swept away by floods. Of course, now that she thought about it, it made sense. Regular houses, land houses, miles from any river, were swept away by floods, let alone riverhouses that were just sitting on the water, waiting for a flood.

"Yes, and you know," continued Nancy, "that was very exciting, too, because my brother who lived on the river had to save us. He had a tug. Oh, in those days this house was miles from here, on another part of the Willamette, back in the city under the Ross Island Bridge. You know that bridge?"

Lazy nodded. It was at least fifteen miles away. "You mean it went that far?"

"Oh no, honey, we were moored not far from there. Anyhow, the flood came and we just started rolling away. We would have crashed right into the bridge . . ."

"You were *in* the house?" This was unbelievable.

"Well, of course we were in the house, dear. We lived in it, just like you."

"Oh of course." Lazy was planning an escape route if the waterline rose more than a foot during any season.

"Anyhow, we just got going and we would have crashed but my brother, the tugboat fella, he saw us and came steaming alongside and he got hold of the house and tied it up with a chain to one of the steel beams under the Ross Island Bridge, and then he went off to save some other houses."

Lazy decided that tugboat people were good friends to have.

"You should get to know the tug people," Nancy said, reading her mind. "They can save your life. Why one time when we were down here on the Channel, there was another flood. A mighty one. All the houseboats broke loose just about the same time. You know, we're all tied together, and we were just starting for the ocean when the tug from the next moorage came tootin' down here and swung around and just held the last houseboat in place. All the other houseboats drifted and banged against that last one, but it was better than drifting and banging down to the ocean. The tug held us until the flood was over and the waterline came down again. Then we tied ourselves back up to the walkway."

"Ocean . . ." Lazy mumbled.

"Yes, right out to sea we would have gone, probably only would have taken a half hour or so given that current. Of course, nowadays you've got that nuclear power plant downriver. Don't want to crash into that!" She laughed.

Lazy frequently remembered the nuclear power plant downriver. On the grounds of the plant, the Brotherhood of Electrical Workers held their annual picnic. "Never attend that," she had cautioned Pubah.

"Don't you worry, I won't," Pubah had promised.

Nancy looked around and patted the stove and refrigerator. "Nice appliances," she said, smiling.

"Thanks."

"Well, I'll be off now. Interesting you have it all one big room out here. We used to have lots of little rooms; it was all divided up, you know, for the kids. My children all grew up in this house."

"Well, we weren't the ones who made it one big room . . ." Lazy began to say, when she noticed that Nancy had crystal teardrops coming down her rosy cheeks and was looking around the room at another life.

"Thank you very much for coming by and telling me all about the

Tug people

21

riverhouse," Lazy said instead. "And thanks for letting your children grow up here. It's a wonderful, adventurous thing to do and not many women would insist on it the way you did."

"Yes!" Nancy was smiling again. "I just insisted and my kids are all strong swimmers and smart about the river." She looked around once more and then said, "I'll be going."

"Goodbye," Lazy said.

Nancy stepped carefully onto the walkway and turned around. "Thanks for letting me stop in." She waved.

When she was gone, Lazy went back inside and looked around the room. "Brave little riverhouse," she said, and thought that she would tell Pubah all the stories that night as they were falling asleep. Then she looked across at the opposite shore and checked the waterline. "Nice and low," she assured herself and poured some tea. "Way below the floodline and no storms coming."

The dog and cats looked at her and came close, assuming she was talking to them about food.

"I'm just saying we're safe today," she told them, "no need to get excited."

She was very excited herself, however, and it took a long time before she could see a thing in her mind's eye except flames shooting up through the fireplace into the sky as the second story blew downriver while the whole Nancy family sat in what they had thought, moments before, was a cozy living room.

"My, my, my," she said to herself.

The Dads
◆ ◆ ◆

Pubah was a tired girl. Up at dawn. Bed at 2 a.m. Many things to do. She had to make phone calls, for instance. She had to make about fifty phone calls every day. Sometimes she had to make phone calls about making phone calls. She had to build buildings too, and do dishes, and help clean up the house; she also had a stained glass lamp she'd been making for two years, and she wanted to play her saxophone as much as possible. She had pictures to draw and things to write down. She had to finish sawing off the front porch and attend meetings. All of this caused a certain exhaustion to creep into her life, but still every night she wanted to talk things over with Lazy LaRue and share things that happened. She wanted to talk about the people she knew and the things they did. Lazy loved to hear everything. She was not quite as busy. Much less so.

One night in bed they snuggled together.

"You know Wayne?" Pubah said sleepily.

"Mmmmm," Lazy said.

"Well, Wayne," Pubah yawned, "Wayne had to do something. Had to clean something up in his past. He stole something."

Big sigh. Lazy snuggled closer.

"What did he steal?" she asked.

"He took some jewelry from his workplace. He works with jewels." She yawned again.

"He took jewelry?" Lazy was shocked. "When?"

"Last year." Pubah's eyes started to close, but she kept on talking. "He wanted to tell his boss and return it."

"Does Sarah know?" Sarah was the woman Wayne lived with.

Pubah nodded. Her eyes were shut now and wouldn't open. "The dads know too," she said.

Lazy thought for a minute. The dads knew. Sarah's dad and Wayne's dad must know.

"Oh," she said solemnly.

"Yeah." Pubah held her closely and breathed in long, even breaths. "One dad was mean but the other one was great."

"Oh?" Lazy wondered. "Which one was mean about it, hers or his?"

Silence.

a certain exhaustion crept into her life

"Pubah, which dad was mean about it, Sarah's or Wayne's?"

Pubah opened her eyes and looked at Lazy. "What?" she asked.

"Well, I just wanted to know, I was just kind of curious, you know, as to which dad was mean and which was great." There was a long pause. "I was just curious about those dads," Lazy said.

"Dads?" Pubah asked, blinking. "There aren't any dads in this story."

"Go to sleep now," Lazy said, putting her arms around Pubah. "Time to go to sleep."

Pubah Prepares for the Brotherhood
◆ ◆ ◆

Pubah was studying for her journeyman's license.

"Journey*person*," Lazy said, but Pubah explained that in the Brotherhood of Electrical Workers they just call everybody a journeyman.

"Well, I think they should change that," Lazy said. "It's outdated."

"It's true that you're living with one of the first American women to be an electrician," smiled Pubah, "so for a while we'll just have to live with our terms in combination with the older ones."

"Journeywoman, then," Lazy asserted.

"Anything you say. By the way, I'm going to need to do a lot of studying for this test. I figure if I study a half hour a day from my U.S.A. Electrical Code Book I'll have the whole thing memorized by January when I take my test."

Lazy made a promise, "I'll remind you to study." It was not an easy promise to keep, as it turned out.

Pubah looked at the terms listed in her code book. "Okay, I know the terms," she said. "Ask them to me."

Lazy asked her, "What is a service drop? A receptacle? A panelboard? A grounder? A header? Hey, this sounds like baseball."

Pubah knew all of the terms.

"I know the terms," she said. "Now for the wiring methods."

Each night, sleepy Pubah sat up in bed reading from her code book and muttering to herself. She printed highly technical information on 3 x 5 cards and took them to work in the morning. "I'll study these while I'm working on the switchgear," she said.

Every day for a week she replenished her supply of 3 x 5 cards covered with electrical code information and studied them while she drilled holes, bent pipe, installed switches, and carried equipment.

The more she studied, the more Lazy was impressed and slacked off in checking up on her. One night she fell asleep while Pubah was looking at her code book and marking things with a yellow marker. Five minutes later she awoke, looked at the clock, and saw Pubah sound asleep. "Wake up," she nudged her. "Remember you have to study for at least half an hour before you go to sleep."

Pubah didn't open her eyes. "Come on, Pubah," Lazy gently shook her.

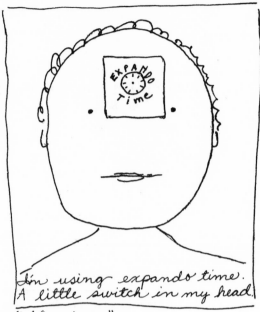

I'm using expando time.
A little switch in my head.

"You've only studied five minutes."

"No. Half hour."

Lazy looked at the clock. "Five minutes."

"I'm using expando time," Pubah told her. "A little switch in my head. I turn it on and five minutes of studying becomes equal to a half hour."

Lazy thought for a moment, then concluded, "Pubah, there's no such thing as expando time."

"There should be," groaned Pubah. "I should invent it."

She opened her eyes and sat up in bed. "Just think," she added, "it could apply to anything. Jogging. Meditation. Yoga. Let's say you were supposed to meditate fifteen minutes a day. With expando time you could do it all in a minute and a half."

Lazy picked up the code book. "What are Class 2, Division 2 locations?"

"Class 2, Division 2 locations," Pubah mumbled, leaning back on her pillow, "in accordance with the provisions of article 1006 . . . ."

In the middle of electricians school, Pubah was nominated for Apprentice of the Year.

She came home horrified and announced it. "I've been nominated for Apprentice of the Year. This is awful," she said, collapsing on the futon. "Now I'll probably have to study even harder."

"It sounds like a great honor to me," Lazy said.

"No. I mean yes. No. I don't know. It is but it would make me, you know, so visible, competing with a bunch of men, bending pipe, installing things while they're timing us. I try to keep a low profile, you know."

Lazy tried to imagine this. "How can you possibly keep a low profile?" she asked. "You're the only woman at work."

"Well, I guess I can't," Pubah conceded. "You know, today I went out on a job to fix some switchgear that was damaged by a fire, and when I came to the plant where it was, the men all took a break and watched me. One came within twenty feet and just stood there, watching the whole time. The rest of them wanted to come that close but they didn't have the . . . you know, the whaddyacall . . ."

Lazy remembered. "Balls?" she offered cheerfully.

"Yeah. Balls. So they watched and when I was finished I had to walk right past this person in order to leave. I went by him and said howdy."

"What did he say?"

"Nothing." Pubah closed her eyes.

They were both sad for a minute. "Then," Pubah continued, "I went back to my workplace and they told me to go upstairs into this big closet where they have the wires for the computer. They got a word processor today and they told me to hook it up. So I was up there and Duffy, one of the warehouse guys, came by and chuckled, 'Stuck in the closet, eh?' It was so, you know, appropriate to say about me at work. He just said it and walked on. I don't even think he knows what that means."

Lazy came over and smoothed Pubah's hair. "Mmmm," she said.

"I just sat in there for a while and stared at nothing. Then I got back to work."

"Would you like to be Apprentice of the Year?" Lazy asked.

Pubah opened her eyes and looked as sincere as Lazy had ever seen her. "I'd like to be a drummer," she said.

Lazy picked up the code book. "When can type RLC cables be used, Pubah?"

"For one- and two-family dwellings," Pubah sighed, "or multifamily dwellings not to exceed . . . ."

Pubah, Jodie, and Lazy LaRue Find a Snake in the River
◆ ◆ ◆

Lazy LaRue, Jodie, and Pubah were crossing the river one day in a canoe. Jodie, Lazy's godchild, liked the canoe and the river very much. It was getting dark. The hot day was ending. The river hardly moved. They paddled near the shore where the cows grazed. They were paddling under a swallow's nest on a piling when Pubah said, "What's that?"

Jodie said, "I don't know."

Lazy looked around. "I don't see anything. Where?"

Jodie and Pubah tried to point and paddle at the same time.

"Right there," they said. "What is that?"

And then Pubah said, "It's a snake!"

Lazy saw it then. It was dark with a red stripe down its back. "Is it poisonous?" Jodie asked.

"I think it's a garter snake," said Pubah.

"Noooo, it isn't," said Jodie. "That's a poisonous snake."

"Well, maybe it is," Lazy thought out loud.

"Oh, it isn't," said Pubah.

"Well, how do you know?" Jodie wondered. "I think it's one of those poisonous racer snakes."

"No," Lazy shook her head, "it isn't. It's a garter snake." She could see it better now that they were close to it.

"Some of those gartner snakes are poisonous," Jodie said, turning all the way around to argue and almost tipping over the canoe. The little snake came right up next to them and stuck out its tongue, then slipped under the canoe and emerged on the other side. It stopped to rest, then slithered on.

They followed it.

Once or twice it stopped and twisted around as though considering going back where it came from. They all wondered how it knew where it was going and why it had started out.

"I know it's poisonous," said Jodie as they paddled away and headed back toward the riverhouse.

Knowledge

♦ ♦ ♦

N ext door to the riverhouse lived a young man who was getting married.

"Married," Lazy glanced at Pubah. "Now there's an interesting idea."

"Hmm," mumbled Pubah.

The young man came to call. "I'm having a party tonight," he told them. "Snake dancer."

"I beg your pardon," Lazy said. "How do you mean, snake dancer?"

"Well," blushed the young man, "I mean there's a dancer coming. It's a stag party and there's just the one, you know, the one dancer."

Lazy didn't quite understand but Pubah said she thought that would be all right. "If that's what you want to do, Willie."

That night Lazy and Pubah fell asleep early. They were asleep with their lips together after many soft kisses. Lazy was dreaming of dolphins swimming in slow circles, then pressing their noses together and swimming again.

Suddenly there was a crashing and many grunts. "Ugh!" "Oooof!"

There was a shout, "Hungh!" And another, "Gargh!" A splash, then "Whoagh, hey! Hey!"

"Vikings!" whispered Pubah, her eyes wide open.

"Yes, Vikings!" Lazy agreed, amazed at how both of them could rise from a dead sleep and enter, without pause, their mutual Scandinavian ancestry.

Vikings

29

More crashes, a whap, then profanity. On and on and on, miles of profanity spoken through watery chokes. "You son of a . . . (bubbling gurgle) . . . you!"

A door slammed.

Pubah got up and peeked out the window.

"There's a Viking in the water," she whispered.

"Oh my," said Lazy from the bed. "Is he drowning?"

"No," Pubah told her. "One of his friends is helping him out."

"A stag?" Lazy wondered.

"Looks like a stag, yes," Pubah said, coming back to bed.

"I hope the snake dancer is all right."

"Oh yeah, she's okay." Pubah seemed to know.

Lazy was surprised. "How do you know? How do you know she's okay? She's just over there with all those stags, all night long."

Pubah closed her eyes. "They have bodyguards."

"Snake dancers?"

"All snake dancers have bodyguards. They bring them to these stag parties."

Pubah was almost asleep but Lazy was wide-eyed with awe. "You know just about everything, don't you, Pubah?"

"Just about," Pubah sighed, pulling Lazy close. "I know about snake dancers anyway."

"Why?" Lazy was truly curious.

"Electricians," Pubah answered and then began to snore.

Lazy had certainly been forced to expand her idea of what an electrician was since Pubah started to become one. No longer were electricians simply people who repaired broken dishwashers, as they had been in Lazy's childhood. No! Electricians were worldly people with a knowledge of life Lazy had never discovered in all the books she had read. Electricians were not only masters of the tangled flow of wires alive with current. They, along with Pubah, put together high-rise apartment houses and wired pieces of machinery as large as barns, all the while discussing the very seamiest side of existence.

She heard the Viking thrash and splash in the water. The stag must be pulling at him. "You're a heavy so-and-so," swore the stag.

"Yeah, well, you ain't such a twig yourself, you know, Donald . . . ."

She heard the ramp sigh with the weight of the wet Viking and the stag leaving.

"They're gone," she whispered to Pubah, who was already quite asleep.

Lazy wondered for a long time about wedding rituals before the dolphins reappeared, coaxing her back with their slow, circular water dance.

Pubah Gets a Bathing Suit, a Straw Hat and Sunglasses

◆ ◆ ◆

Glamorous Pubah hid her light under a bushel until the day she got the bathing suit, the straw hat, and the sunglasses. Everywhere Pubah went she looked nice and cute and clean. She had reddish, brownish, blondish hair always shining, clear skin, and her eyes were dark sparkles. She was just fine until she bought these items and thereby changed the world by becoming irresistible.

The bathing suit plunged down and at the same time pushed out and up, causing Pubah, with her hourglass figure, to look just like a movie star. Especially with that hat and those glasses. Lazy couldn't keep her eyes off. Strangers honked and waved. Tugboats tooted, etc. Nothing was ever the same again.

Glamorous Pubah

31

Spiderwebs
◆ ◆ ◆

Everything was going well at the riverhouse. Summer warmed the tile floors. Doors were swung open wide to let the cool breeze in from the river. There were no screens so sometimes birds flew in and flew out again. Lazy might spend a whole afternoon telepathically informing a trembling swallow about the variety of exits it could take.

"Window over there!" she would beam from a distance at the little bird, admiring wings of deep blue satin and worrying as the orange breast nearly popped with the thud of the heart. "Door! Door! It's open! Go to the door!" she ordered meditatively.

If she could keep the cats away, this method usually worked. If not, she had to trap the bird and carry it to freedom herself.

On one of their first summer evenings in the riverhouse, Lazy and Pubah sat on their deck and noticed why the swallows liked flying around their house. There were nearly fifty spiderwebs between them and the river and each web held a fat, juicy, hairy and lively spider. Once their eyes focused on these visitors from nature, they could not behold them in peace.

"Brooms!" Pubah cried. "Or mops! Get mops!" They rushed into the house and ran out again waving cleaning implements at the twilight sky. Within moments they had destroyed every single spiderweb. The spiders went scurrying away and Lazy and Pubah sat down, breathing hard from the attack.

Several times they repeated to one another, "Did you see how big those spiders were?"

These were city women. Fifty spiders did not belong hanging from the rooftop of a house, to their minds. Fifty spiders belonged on the riverbank crawling through the grass. "Back to earth, creatures." Lazy called after them.

They smiled and shook hands with each other and decided to go to sleep on the futon. It was a warm night. They left the windows and doors open. Just as they began to doze off, they heard the buzzing. It was quiet enough at first, one lonely mosquito looking for a taste of blood, but within minutes it became a roar of bloodthirsty attackers. Lazy and Pubah rushed around shutting doors and windows, but it still took most of the night to fend off the mosquitoes that had already entered.

Toward dawn Pubah muttered, "I guess we've learned our lesson."

Lazy could not remember a lesson. All she wanted was sleep, delicious sleep, with no buzzing and no itching. "What lesson?"

"The spiders," Pubah reminded her. "They kept the mosquitoes from us."

"Oh, precious spiders!" Lazy raced to the window. "Come back! We're sorry."

They needn't have worried. Ancient and tolerant, the spiders had once again spun fifty webs by sunset. Lazy and Pubah sat on their deck drinking iced peppermint tea. They watched the spiders catching hundreds upon hundreds of mosquitoes.

Lazy took Pubah's hand as they gazed into the webworks.

"Happy, darling?" she asked.

"Happy," Pubah told her.

Pubah Gets a Godchild

◆ ◆ ◆

Pubah was worried. She was supposed to get a godchild any day but she kept not hearing about it. She was supposed to get it from her best friend in Sweden who was to give birth to it. She waited for a phone call but it didn't come.

She started to cry.

"She's dead!" she cried to Lazy LaRue, who didn't know what she was talking about.

"I know she is, I know it! She died in childbirth!"

Then Lazy knew what she was talking about. She comforted her and knew what was needed. "Let's call her," she suggested.

"No, I can't," Pubah told Lazy. "I can't hear that she's dead."

Crying, crying, crying all the time.

So Lazy LaRue called Sweden, dialing fast.

"You have to dial really fast," Pubah told her, hanging onto her shoulder, "or you'll get some other country."

Lazy found out that the godchild was born and it was a girl and the name was Gaia.

"Gaia, Gaia, Gaia, Gaia!" Pubah jumped around the kitchen of the riverhouse. "Gaia, Gaia, Gaia, Gaia!"

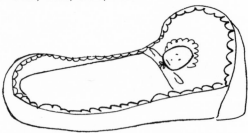

Complaining
◆ ◆ ◆

Y ou don't have it any harder than I do," Pubah began the argu-
ment with Lazy who was complaining about something. "Stop
complaining."

"I like to complain."

"Well, it's not inspiring."

Lazy considered. "Perhaps it's not." Then, unwilling to be vulnerable,
"You can inspire yourself, however."

This time, Pubah considered. "Yes, I can," she said, and then, unwilling to surrender, "If you keep this up I'll have to inspire myself, won't I?"

Lazy watched them tumble into the morass. "Me?" she asked feigning
bewilderment. "I'm not doing anything."

"You're complaining all the time."

"I complained once."

"Did not."

"Did."

"Well, when you complain it takes forever. It takes up all of forever and
eternity. You don't have it any harder than anybody else. Nobody has it
any harder than anybody else."

Lazy could not be still. "Oh that's a ridiculous thing to say." She
slammed her fist down.

"It is not." Pubah got up and walked away.

Lazy followed. "It is."

"Is not."

"Oh, Pubah, it's absurd. Listen to yourself. Nobody has it any harder
than anybody else. How can you say that?"

Pubah was firm. "Because it's true."

"Oh, it is *not!*" And on and on and on and on and on and on and on
and on like that.

Pubah Has a Dream
◆ ◆ ◆

Pubah had dreams that she liked to talk about in the car when Lazy drove her into the city to work. Lazy liked to listen.

"I know what I'm going to do when I'm turned out," Pubah said. She was always talking about turning out because that's what electricians do and she was becoming an electrician. "I'm going straight to Europe."

"Oh?" said Lazy.

"Yes. I'm going to get on a boat and just go. You too. We're going to drink coffee all over Europe." Then she pointed at a small dark car zipping through the rain and said, "Oh, I want one of those. Maybe I'll buy a Fiat."

She thought she needed a car.

The next day, driving through the rain again, on the way to work again, Pubah said, "As soon as I turn out, I'm going to art school."

"Oh?" Lazy said, looking off through the wet morning imagining Pubah with paintbrushes and a big canvas and a teacher standing behind her.

She and Lazy drove back and forth to work.

36

"Yes, I'm going to the museum art school and I'll be an artist. Oh, look at that," she said, pointing to a Japanese truck. "Maybe I'll get one of those."

The next day she said, "I'm going to have my own construction firm."

"Really?" said Lazy.

"Yes, all women," Pubah declared. "Wouldn't that be great? And I'll only work when I want to. Oh, I might have to get one of those. Look!" She pointed to a blue Volvo just like the red one she was riding in.

The next day she said, "You know what I'm going to do when I turn out?"

"No, what?" asked Lazy.

"I'm going to buy a horse farm. We'll just ride horses all day. Oh my, look at that car. That's the car I want." She pointed at a little red MG splashing through the watery streets of Portland.

At night she colored musculature in her anatomy coloring book and let Lazy LaRue snuggle up next to her. "I love you," she said.

China
◆ ◆ ◆

L azy LaRue and Pubah were curled up on the futon in the liv-
ingroom of the riverhouse. It was a soft breezy night and they
were looking out through the big window at the blue herons.
The large birds swooped down along the river searching for food,
then lifted themselves gracefully into the sky again. Occasionally, a slow
boat would sail by and cause the silver water to gently rock the
riverhouse.

"Well," sighed Pubah, "I'll be going to China soon."

Lazy, who was prone to hysteria, jumped up and looked at Pubah
curled up there on the futon like a normal person who had just done
nothing more than mention what a nice day it was.

"China?" Lazy stared at her. "Did you say China? Did I hear you say
that? You don't mean the country, China, do you, the one that's over on
the other side of the world across the ocean? You don't mean the country
where the Chinese live and where everybody speaks Chinese and they
have red silk shoes on the children and do exercises in the factory yards
and ride bicycles? You don't mean that China, do you? That's not the
China you mean. You don't mean the China where there's a big wall that
a lot of people built and there was a revolution and a red book and then
they put up all the pictures of Mao and had thoughts for the day and
then they took down all the pictures of Mao and stopped having
thoughts for the day, where Jayne Meadows was born and her sister
Audrey Meadows, and Jayne Meadows was later on "I've Got a Secret"
and she married Steve Allen who, after many years of searching for his
lost brother, found him somewhere in the southern United States and
Audrey was on the Jackie Gleason show with the circle on the floor of
dancing girls' legs—you can't mean that China, right? You don't mean
the China where there are 700 million people and they don't need any
more and they're starting to wear blue jeans and there are rolling hills?
That's not the China you're going to, is it?"

"Oh yes," cried Pubah, "that's exactly the China I'm going to. You
know so much about it already. You're such a smart person, Lazy. You're
as smart as a Ph.D."

At moments like this, Lazy wondered what particular brand of cotton
Pubah had stuffed between her little ears that she could attribute the

Birthplace of Jayne & Audrey Meadows

Jayne Meadows and her sister Audrey Meadows.

most ordinary information to above average intelligence.

"I just don't feel that smart," Lazy said. "I just think we must be talking about two different Chinas because if you go to China you would be very far away from me."

"Oh no, not at all." Pubah sat up and gave Lazy a big hug. "I wouldn't be far away from you at all. I'd be right next to you."

"Oh, really?" Lazy looked at her. "And how would that be so?"

"Well, because you'd be right next to me in China."

"But what would I do in China? By the way, Pubah, what are you going to do in China?"

"I'm going to be an electrician in China."

"An electrician? Don't they have some of those already?"

"Yes," Pubah told her, "but many of the men at my work talk about going there so they must need more electricians. All the men at my work do very creative things with their taxes and many are going to China. They all have boats. They want to go to China because you can get paid a lot of money there and there are no taxes and it's an interesting place to live."

Lazy pictured boatloads and boatloads of electricians sailing across the sea to China. She saw them grabbing money out of the hands of people who had blown fuses in their houses. She saw them stuffing money into their shirts, their toolbelts, under their hardhats.

Suddenly Lazy wanted to go for a walk and think about everything in her entire life. "I have no doubt that it's very interesting there," she said to Pubah, "but if you'll excuse me, I have to go out now and think about everything in my entire life."

39

"Oh, Lazy," Pubah pleaded, "don't go because I said we're going to China."

But it was too late. Lazy put on her purple sweatshirt, her jeans and her sandals. "Well," she explained, "sometimes I feel like I'd just like to hide out in this riverhouse, you know, Pubah, and you come up with such extreme ideas and I just find I have to think about it all."

Pubah smiled. "Yeah, when we're in China you probably won't ever want to leave there, either."

Lazy pictured herself in a riverhouse on the Yangtze identical to the one they now occupied. "Somehow," she said, "I think I'd want to leave that one. After all, I'm kind of busy to go to China. What about the novels I have planned? If I went to China I'd have to write about China. I don't have time. You don't think about these things, Pubah."

"No," Pubah agreed. "I don't think about these things."

"What about my dog, for example? Can she go? And my friends? What about my friends?"

"There sure are a lot of things to worry about," Pubah nodded.

"I'll say!" Lazy said, going out the door. "And I'm going to worry about all of them. See you later."

"Later," said Pubah.

The Jackie Gleason Show

Some Good Friends Leave Oregon
◆ ◆ ◆

Catlin and Al said they were moving to Seattle.

"Well, goodbye then!" Lazy was angry. "Goodbye, goodbye, goodbye!"

Lazy hated it when anybody left. She took it as a personal affront. What had she done wrong anyway? Nobody could tell her.

"They're just moving," Pubah explained. "You didn't do anything wrong."

"Well, let them go then," Lazy shouted. "Go! Leave my presence!" At times of sorrow, Lazy became unaccountably queenly.

"Everybody's going sometime," Pubah consoled her. "We're all going to go somewhere, sometime."

"Silence!" Lazy commanded. "I'm not going anywhere, ever. Never! Never ever ever!"

She loved Catlin and Al so much and their little talky daughter, Rosita, who knew all the angels personally.

"You're going because you want something better," Lazy accused Al.

"I'm going because I'm going." Al was logical.

"Me too," Catlin blinked back her tears. "Goin' cause I'm goin'."

"Oh, for heaven's sake, you sound like hoboes," Lazy told them. "This is real life. This ain't no freight train."

Everybody nodded tolerantly. Lazy had a yen to be poetic.

"I'm mad!" she hollered. "I hate this!"

They allowed she did and they all saw, including her, that there was nothing she could do.

"Nothing I can do," she said sadly, sitting down next to Pubah.

"Nope," Pubah put her arms around Lazy. "Nothing to do."

Hornets

◆ ◆ ◆

Lazy sat in the back room at her desk, thinking about writing. She was thinking about writing something so great that people would weep when they touched the pages. She wanted to push her readers out to the very edges of whatever they thought they were or could be and demand even more. She sat thinking, imagining, fondling her favorite coffee mug, when a hornet flew in. Quickly, she jumped up, ran to the kitchen and found a jar. Within moments she had saved the hornet and set free its furious buzzing body into the air over the water. Pleased with herself, she returned to her room and sat down again.

Another hornet came in. Then another. Followed by another. This was too much. How could she write something truly great with hornets pestering her? What if she got stung and died?

Once again she got out the jar and caught the hornets and threw them out the door.

"I hope you'll remember this," she called after them. "I could have just sprayed you with something, you know."

By the time she got back to her room, there were more hornets. In fact, as she opened the door, a hornet buzzed the top of her head.

Pubah came rushing in the front door, just off work. Lazy went to the kitchen to greet her. "There are hornets coming in all the time, Pubah."

"Don't get stung," Pubah warned her. "It really hurts when a hornet stings you."

"Well, I don't want to get stung."

Pubah had to hurry. She was going somewhere to lead a meeting. As she stripped off her workclothes and stepped into the shower, she asked a question, "Is it earlier or later, Lazy?"

Lazy stood outside the shower and thought for a minute. It could be earlier. On the other hand, it might be later.

"Later," she guessed.

"Later?"

"What are we talking about, Pubah?"

"In New York. I have to call there. Is it earlier or later?"

Lazy was pleased that she'd had the right answer to begin with. "Later," she said. "About those hornets . . . I think it's pretty serious. We need screens."

Pubah screamed. "EEEEEEEEEEK!"

Lazy jumped. "What are you doing?"

"You said we need screams. I'm screaming. EEEEEEK!" As loud as she could.

"No, we need screens. Mesh screens, that you put over doors and windows."

"Oh, yeah," Pubah called loudly through the pouring water. "Yeah, that makes more sense. I thought it was kind of an old-fashioned request. Screaming. But I was willing to do it."

"Pubah, life is not a comedy show."

"It isn't?"

Pubah stepped out of the shower and ran, dripping, to the telephone to dial New York. "I have to order pages for my timekeeping system," she explained to Lazy, who was looking at the ceiling upon which crawled several hornets. "I'm almost out of pages."

After a few moments, she hung up the phone. "Do you think they're on their lunch break? They're not answering. Let's see, it's five o'clock here . . . ."

"Pubah," Lazy looked at her and folded her arms across her chest. "It's later. Later. Remember?"

"Here?"

"There. They're all reading or eating or making love. Maybe they're at a movie or a play. There's a good play I read about today in the *New Yorker* . . . maybe they're . . . ."

"I got it. I got it," Pubah said, then she jumped aside as a hornet flew past. "EEEEEEEK!" she screamed.

Lazy shook her head. "Yeah. Eek is right."

The Tile

♦ ♦ ♦

Jodie and Lazy made a request of Pubah. "Tell us a story about when you were young." The three of them and Carson, the whippet, were all sunbathing on a bed of logs tied together downstream from the riverhouse.

"Okay," said Pubah. "I'll tell you about the tile." Pubah's eyes were closed, her face turned toward the sun.

"The tile?" Jodie wrinkled up her nose and sat up to listen. "Well," she urged, "what about it? What happened with the tile?"

Pubah began with a smile. "I was home alone."

Lazy closed her eyes and relaxed, listening.

"I was cooking eggs," Pubah said. "Boiling them . . . ." She paused.

"Yes, yes!" Jodie was impatient.

"But I got interested in something else. I was in Junior High, a little older than you." She opened her eyes and looked at the ten-year-old Jodie, who nodded, "and I couldn't remember that I was boiling eggs if I had something else going on. I was busy upstairs and pretty soon I heard a BANG! Then a CRASH! I rushed to the kitchen. The eggs had exploded. They were all over the ceiling, and the worst thing was that the pan had been blown off the stove by the explosion and had landed in the middle of the room and made a big black mark on the tile."

Jodie clasped her hands over her mouth. By now, Lazy was sitting up, her eyes open.

"Yeah." Pubah nodded at them both. "Serious. I could not get that black mark off no matter how hard I scrubbed it or what I scrubbed it with. Then," she tapped her noggin, "idea!"

"What?" Jodie wondered.

"I remembered that my own father, who was going to be very upset if he saw this and who would be home soon with my mother, had put those tiles down himself." She jumped up on the logs. "Rush, rush, rush down to the garage. Dig dig. Scramble! Dig around some more . . . ." By now Pubah was reliving the very core of the experience. She was standing on the logs searching an invisible garage. "Aha!" She grabbed something out of the air. "The tiles!" She held one up and beamed at it.

"I raced back up to the kitchen, got a knife, took off the black-marked tile and realized there had to be something to make the new tile stick in

The eggs had exploded

place so . . . back to the garage to the can area. Cans and cans and cans. Turpentine. Cleaning fluid. Paint, paint, paint, paint. Paint thinner. Paint remover. Varnish. Maple wood stain. Carpenter's glue . . . . Linoleum tile fixative . . . that's it! I grabbed it."

Again she grabbed the air. "And I raced back upstairs but as soon as I came into the kitchen I noticed something." Her face fell. It looked to Jodie and Lazy as though it would fall right on the logs.

"What? What?" By now they were racing ahead of the story, trying to make up the details. "The tile was gone!" Jodie said with alarm.

"No," Pubah shook her head. "The tile was there. It was just so . . . so clean. All the other tiles around it had been walked on for five years. They were kind of yellow and smudged. So I had to have another idea and fast. I took the tile outside and smeared it with dirt and walked on it in the driveway—back and forth, back and forth, stomping!" She stomped to demonstrate. "Trying to get it five years worth of dirty in five minutes. It was almost time for my parents to come home. Any minute I would hear their car."

"Hurry!" Jodie and Lazy shouted.

"Yes! So I picked up the tile and ran upstairs and glued it in place. Then I picked up the can of glue and ran to the stairs to go down to the garage and, oh, no! The glue spilled!"

Lazy and Jodie started to laugh. They couldn't help it, even though Pubah's eyes were wide with horror.

"GLOP! GLOP! Down the stairs, out the front of the garage, down the driveway, down the hill, the very hill my own parents would be driving up any moment, so I ran and got the hose and sprayed everything. Sprayed the stairway, sprayed the pavement, sprayed down the hill as far as my hose could go. It was a white river now, wide and sticky but the glue was water soluble and was slowly disappearing. Another hour or so of water would have done it, but I saw my parents come driving up the hill. I ran to the middle of the driveway and sprayed the glue some more. I tried to behave innocently. 'Oh hi.'" Pubah waved innocently at a passing motorboat.

"My mother said, 'What's that?' I answered: 'I spilled some milk.' My mother said, 'Oh.' I followed her anxiously upstairs. As soon as she entered the kitchen she pointed at the shining new white tile in the middle of the room and said, 'What's that?' " Pubah sat down, dejected. "She noticed it right away. It was just sparkling white."

"What did you do?" Lazy asked her.

Pubah shrugged. "I told the truth. I said, 'Mom, the eggs exploded.' "

Jodie asked, "Were you punished?"

"No. Not that time. That time they just spoke firmly. I was punished for other things, other times, of course."

Pubah looked at Lazy. "Did you ever do anything like that when you were young?"

Lazy thought. "Well, once I took the faucet handles from the upstairs bathroom and left the water running. My brother was outside and he needed the faucet handles. He asked me to get them, so I did."

"Gosh!" Jodie was amazed. "What happened?"

"The water ran and ran. Made a big watermark on the ceiling."

Lazy leaned back down on the logs and stretched her thin body out to the sun. "Never got punished," she said.

"Do you mean you never got punished for anything?" Jodie and Pubah were incredulous.

"Never. Never. Never got punished for anything."

"I don't think that's good for a child." Jodie looked serious.

"Worked fine for me," Lazy LaRue said. "I turned out fine."

"*Never* got punished!" Jodie and Pubah couldn't believe it. They stretched their bodies out to the sun again too.

"I get grounded," Jodie said.

"Yeah," Pubah was sympathetic. "I used to get grounded too."

"I never got grounded once," Lazy said. "Not once."

"Oh, you be quiet now," Pubah warned her.

"Yeah," Jodie agreed.

"Never punished," Lazy said again, quietly. "For anything." Softly, "Never, never, never . . . ."

"Quiet!"

Pubah's Workload
◆ ◆ ◆

Lazy was always amazed at the things Pubah remembered to take to work with her every morning. Pubah was not terribly alert in the mornings. Sometimes she got up and said nothing. Once she got up and said, "So many mornings, all in a row. Why?" But she always managed to remember everything.

She rushed around getting things together that she would need for work and for after work. Lazy wanted to help but couldn't imagine Pubah's schedule and so she stood by and tried to be cheerful while Pubah went through her closet, her drawers, and the cupboards.

When it was finally time for Pubah to leave it was only seven o'clock in the morning, but she had enough things with her to last until midnight. On easy days she went out the door with her purse, her thermos, her lunchbox, and her timekeeping system, but many days she had a meeting to attend at night so she had to take clothes into town with her too. That way she did not have to drive all the way back home to change. On those days she added to her cargo not only something to wear to a meeting, but also shoes and nylons, which she carried in an orange pack, and a green bag that contained her toiletries. When she went to seminars on how to transform the quality of life on earth or new ideas for solar projects, she added notebooks and binders and workbooks.

"Goodbye," she called to Lazy as she trudged up the ramp.

"Goodbye," Lazy called into the morning mist.

When Pubah came home late at night she was carrying too many things to get in the door. Lazy could hear her step on the ramp and bump against the door, then fumble for her keys. Lazy always got up to let her in. There was Pubah, the very woman who had left that morning as a construction worker, now in heels and swell clothes.

"Home," Pubah said with a smile. "Home at last." And came back into the house to put things away and start all over again in the morning.

Gaia Arrives in the U.S.
and Takes Command
◆ ◆ ◆

Gaia, Pubah's godchild, did not arrive in the United States until she was nearly three and aware of the earth goddess meaning of her name. She had fine blonde hair and wore rugged European toddler clothes of bright colors. She also wore white clogs with roses on the toes.

She had a great deal to say and didn't hesitate to speak her mind. Her parents, a Swede and an American, looked on adoringly.

"I want sand!" she commanded, so her father took Pubah's yellow pickup truck to the Columbia River and filled the back end with sand.

When Pubah came to play in Gaia's sandbox with her, the godchild noticed that the godmother spilled sand onto the ground. "Don't spill the sand!" she ordered. "Or I won't have any left and we have to go for a long ride again."

Pubah obeyed.

Gaia liked to go to a restaurant called Old Wives' Tales because the restaurant had a special room for children to play in while adults ate. When invited to other restaurants, she declined.

"What is it you don't like about those other restaurants?" Lazy asked her.

"Sit and sit and sit and sit and sit and sit and sit!" the little goddess explained. "I don't like it!"

She spoke a mixture of American and Swedish. "Hey you guys, close the dorren!" she might say.

She liked to talk to Pubah on the phone. "She's my best friend," Gaia informed her mother, who herself had once been Pubah's best friend.

Lazy noticed that Gaia was one of the few people on the planet who had more energy and more ideas than Pubah.

"Let's do this! You hold that! Swing me! Push me! Rock me! Read to me! Let's run now! Pick me up! Tie this! Buckle this! Tickle me! Give me juice! Make me lunch! Hold me upside down! Now!"

One night Lazy picked Pubah up after she had spent a day with Gaia. Pubah could hardly keep her eyes open. The child had pushed her to the limit of her abundant energy.

Lazy had to buckle her seat belt for her.

"We played in the sandbox," Pubah said, "and went to the park and then we did some dancing, followed by band practice. Sally and Mally were there but they didn't do much. I had to do everything."

Sally and Mally were Gaia's invisible friends.

"I carried her on my shoulders for at least six hours . . ."

Suddenly Pubah was asleep and Lazy drove in silence along the river road until they turned down the hill, drove past the wrecking yard and pulled into the parking lot.

"I love her so much," Pubah said, eyes barely open, as she marched down the ramp to bed.

Yancy Comes Visiting on a Sailboat

◆ ◆ ◆

Pubah and Lazy, drowsy and hot, had purchased Perrier and lemons but were too demented by heat to put the two together and refresh themselves.

"I don't want any really," Lazy said, standing in front of the refrigerator. She came and sat down on the futon. A cat, stretched to its limit, would not move over so she and Pubah had to sit close to each other.

"Don't sit so close, please. It's too hot," Pubah murmured in a cranky sort of way.

Lazy, just as cranky, suggested that the cat ought to move. "Move, Max!"

Max did not even open his slitty eyes to acknowledge the order. It was too hot to fight, with a cat or each other. Outside sailboats streamed by and Pubah commented on their peacefulness, then picked up a book called *Synergetics*, wiped the sweat from her brow and began to read.

A few moments later Lazy heard a scuffle and shouts outside.

"What's outside our door, Pubah?" She was alarmed at such noises on a day that demanded stillness.

Pubah did not look up from her book. "The whole world, Lazy."

The voices got loud. "Wait! Hey, now, give me a break! Look out! Everybody push!"

Pubah and Lazy looked at each other, jumped up and ran to the deck of the riverhouse. Next door several other houseboat owners were leaning out from Willie's deck, pushing the bow of a small sailboat away. The boat had come within half an inch of ramming through Willie's 8' by 8' picture window and was stopped only by human strength. The bodies, now parallel to the water, hands on the bow, had calm voices coming from them. "There now, take it easy. We've got it."

Pubah and Lazy were stunned to hear the next voice, that of the sailor. "I'm not even going here," it called over the strained muscular bodies. "I'm going there, to Pubah and Lazy's house."

a cat, stretched to its limit ...

50

"I don't know how to sail this thing yet".

They looked at the lone sailor and saw that it was their friend, Yancy Dalloway, standing up tall in the boat. "And there they are now!" Yancy shouted. "Hi! Hi you guys!"

Lazy and Pubah started to laugh. "Yancy," Pubah shouted, "I didn't know you had a sailboat."

"Just got it today," Yancy called back, her big grin splashing across a sunburned face. "I've been out all morning in it and I love it. Boy, I wasn't sure I could find you two from the waterside of things but it was easy. I remembered you telling me about the little island in front of your house with all the ducks on it and, well, here I am and there you are."

The neighbors, now nearly vertical again, were gently pulling in the boat to tie it up.

"No," Yancy called to them. "Over there. I want to go to their house."

Pubah gave a small wave to the neighbors. "She wants to come to our house."

Their neighbor, Willie, threw the rope to Pubah. "Here you go then," he said. "We'll get back to our card game. I'm sure glad I have a picture window so I could see this thing coming." Then he smiled. "Or maybe I'm not so glad. 'Nice boat,' was my first thought, and my next thought was 'LOOK OUT!' "

Yancy thought this was funny. "Lucky you guys were in there. I don't know how to sail this thing yet."

The neighbors, sailors all, went right back to their card game without further comment and Yancy came inside the riverhouse after tying her boat up to a post on the front porch.

"Well now!" she said in her large voice as she stood in front of the refrigerator. "How are you anyhow? Got a beer? What's this? Perrier?

You're kidding. Can I have some? How come you don't drink beer like normal people on a day like this? Isn't it hot?"

With a glass of Perrier in hand she walked to the futon, pushed Max off, and sat down. "There you go, fella," she said. "The floor's cooler, you know. Heat rises." Then she smiled. "Well?"

Pubah and Lazy loved Yancy. She was big-boned, large-hearted, beautiful, strong, and easy to please. "I like this place," she told them as she looked around, and they accepted the compliment. "Fixer-upper, huh?"

Yancy was a carpenter. She and Pubah sometimes took their breaks together if they were building something in the city. They had to eat their meals in half an hour so they ate fast and talked and laughed about whatever had happened at work that morning.

Anything Pubah said about work made Yancy laugh and anything Yancy said had the same effect on Pubah. They especially liked to make comments about being women in the trades.

"Women in the trades!" they guffawed together. "Pioneers!"

Today Yancy had another construction story. "You know what we were doing the other day?" she began.

"No, what?" Pubah asked, already laughing.

"Well, the construction company I work for got the bid on the parking structure at the new shopping center."

"Yeah?"

Lazy was worried because Yancy's stories about construction often turned out to be like surgeons' stories about lost sharp instruments at the end of operations.

"We've been over there a few months," Yancy went on. "You know they bid real low to get the thing and they're pressing us all the time—hurry up, hurry up! The materials are really bad, low quality. I don't know . . . I pick some of that stuff up and I'm afraid to put a hammer to it. So the other day we were pounding away and you know how at four o'clock sharp everybody just drops it? Just slam! Tools in the belt, belt slung into the back of the pickup and then you drive off?"

"Yeah?"

"We walked away from it as usual and were just getting to the belt-in-the-back-of-the-pickup part when we heard a horrendous noise. I mean it was like the end of the world. First a kind of creak and then a crash that sounded like an airplane had hit something solid. We turned around and the whole corner of the parking lot, the thing we'd been working on for weeks, had just fallen in. Flat! Tons of wood and cement!"

Pubah had tears running from her eyes. Lazy had never seen her laugh quite so hard. As far as Lazy was concerned it was a frightening story. She ventured into Yancy's laughter, "Anybody hurt?"

"No, no," Yancy shook her head as she laughed. "Luckily we can't wait to get out of there . . . ."

Lazy poured herself a glass of mineral water and downed it.

Yancy finally stopped laughing and stood up to leave. "Well, I think I'll motor on out of here. I don't know how this dang sailing thing works and it's too windy for me to figure it out today. Don't want to upset your neighbors again." She slapped Lazy on the back. "They're probably just getting over their scare."

Pubah and Lazy went out to the porch and hugged Yancy goodbye.

"Thanks for all the mineral water."

Pubah smiled. "Thanks for that great story about the parking lot falling in."

"Plenty more where that came from," Yancy assured her.

Lazy looked up and thanked the clouds she was not in construction work.

Yancy got in the sailboat and turned on the motor. "Well, goodbye!" she called. The neighbors were waving goodbye to her, too. Their card game was breaking up and they were all on Willie's deck looking out at the river.

Slowly Yancy's boat started pulling out onto the water. "Thanks again," she called.

"You're sure welcome," they called back.

"Thanks for stopping me from crashing through the window," she shouted to the neighbors.

"Any time," they shouted back cheerfully, as though it were likely to happen again.

"Bye!" she waved.

"Bye!" they waved, and it was on one of those "byes," perhaps the third or fourth "bye," that Pubah noticed something.

"Oh no!"

Lazy knew it was something serious because Pubah jumped forward and was making rapid motions with her hands over something on the deck, yet she was laughing at the same time. It was confusing.

"Wait, Yancy!" Pubah called, but Yancy was grinning widely and waving at everybody in all the houseboats and calling out more "byes."

Pubah's hands moved furiously. Lazy decided, reluctantly, to step forward and see what she was doing and saw Pubah tearing at the knot on the rope which secured Yancy's sailboat to the post on the front porch of the riverhouse. Just at the last possible second, Pubah pulled the stubborn knot open and threw the rope onto the water.

"Quite the sailor," Lazy said of Yancy, who, oblivious to the near tragedy, was basking in her new-found popularity at the houseboat moorage, waving energetically at houseboat owners and other sailors.

"Happy girl," Pubah said of her as she motored away.

"That was some visitor," Willie called over.

When Yancy was almost out of sight Pubah pointed at the post that held the roof and porch together. "Just saved us some money there," she

53

said with pride to Lazy. Lazy looked up and noticed that she was right. Had the post gone, the roof would have collapsed.

"That Yancy sure has a way with structures," Lazy observed, "and narrow escapes."

Pubah's Theory About Parents and Children and the Issue of Time
◆ ◆ ◆

Gaia had a best friend, Brenna, and they liked to dress alike and do things together and do things with Pubah. Gaia and Brenna had identical dresses made by Brenna's mother. Gaia's dress was red and Brenna's blue. The dresses had wide shoulder straps and butterflies and flowers on them. Whenever they went on an outing they wore their bear packs. Brenna had a koala bear pack and Gaia had a brown bear pack. The fuzzy bears' extremities came over their shoulders and under their arms and the bears' heads turned to the sides.

One day, arrayed in this fashion with the addition of a lot of dirt from Brenna's backyard, they greeted Pubah when she came to see them. They asked if she would take them to the park and then to another park with special swings and then to eat and then to the big park, Laurelhurst, to feed the ducks. Pubah looked at her watch. She knew Gaia's parents were coming to Brenna's house to pick up their daughter at six o'clock. It was five-fifteen when she looked at her watch so she said, "We can't do all those things. We can do two of those things. What will those two things be?"

Gaia and Brenna looked at each other. "Swings and ducks!"

"Okay, but we have to hurry."

"Hurry! Hurry!" Gaia and Brenna raced to the car. They went to the first park and swang and swang on the special tire swings. "Hurry, hurry!" Brenna shouted as she leaped off the swing. "It's time to go."

They got in the car again and started to drive toward Laurelhurst Park, but Gaia remembered, "We don't have anything to feed the ducks!"

"Oh, goodness," Pubah said and turned the corner, went around the block and back in the direction of a store. "We have to hurry."

They pulled up in front of the store and they all rushed inside. Pubah got the bread while Gaia and Brenna ran down the aisle and snatched up some stickers for their Barbie sticker books. "Quick!" They ran back to the car and drove on to Laurelhurst Park, jumped out, and rushed into the greenery.

"How much time do we have?" Gaia wanted to know.

"Five more minutes," Pubah said, breathless behind them. They found the big pond where a hundred ducks were basking in the sun.

"Ducks, come here!" the children called. The ducks heard them. They came flapping and flying and paddling toward the two little girls and the woman, who were all tossing bread onto the surface of the water as fast as they could. The ducks picked up on the frenzy and stepped on one another's heads and bumped and banged together as they went after the bread.

"Time?" Gaia asked.

"Time to go," Pubah told them as the ducks swarmed upon them. They threw the last crumbs into the crowd and raced up the hill to the car, arriving home just as Gaia's parents drove up to fetch her.

Late that night Pubah told Lazy she had a new theory about children and parents and the issue of time.

She told Lazy all about her outing with Gaia and Brenna and then said, "You know how parents come late to things and say, 'well, it was the kids, you know how kids are' . . . you know that phenomenon?"

"Mmmmm." Lazy remembered parents drifting into events later than non-parents, not always, but often, and mumbling about children.

"Well, I think it's the parents who are slow, not the children," Pubah said, sinking into a chair. "Kids are fast. Parents, to be honest, should say 'I'm late because it took me lots of time to get my kids to slow down.'"

Pubah yawned and stretched. "Yep, that's what I think."

"That's an interesting theory. Why don't you bring it up to the parents you know?"

Pubah closed her eyes. "Never."

"Why not?"

"Too dangerous."

"Children forever would love you."

"Not worth it." Pubah smiled and fell asleep.

An Anniversary
◆ ◆ ◆

I'm the kind of person who likes flowers," Pubah said a few days before her anniversary with Lazy. "I'm a romantic sort of person," she went on. "Flowers bring me in touch with my true self."

Lazy watched Pubah writing checks to pay bills and got the hint. "You know," Pubah went on, "there are a lot of bills here. We have bills for clothes I don't even like that we had to buy to appear in public. We have bills for eye testing and teeth cleaning. It's not a romantic thing, paying bills."

"Absolutely not." Lazy saw how mundane it was.

Moments later Pubah looked up and said, "But don't buy me any flowers, all right? Flowers are too expensive."

On the day of their anniversary, while Pubah was at work, Lazy took a break from writing a story and sat with her feet in the cool river reminiscing about their early times together. Lazy and Pubah had liked each other from the moment they met. On that historic day, Lazy was wearing tight blue jeans and a turtleneck, although it was early summer, and Pubah wore striped overalls and a white shirt open wide at the neck. Lazy had short black hair and Pubah had long blonde hair, parted on the side so that much of it fell over one of her dark eyes.

To Lazy these eyes were most attractive. They reminded her of the fertile brown soil in her old country, Iowa. She had a brief moment of thinking, as she looked at this new friend, that she could plant herself in those eyes and flourish.

They immediately started into a conversation about hiking boots and how to keep the leather watertight. They asked each other Oregon questions such as, "Tried mink oil?" And: "What about goose grease?"

In these olden days when Pubah and Lazy were just getting to know each other, they lived in another part of town in separate houses. Pubah lived in an old Victorian house in southeast Portland. She invited Lazy to visit. Lazy noted that Pubah's house had tools hanging all over the walls. Drawings she had done were pinned up everywhere. She also had a lot of raingear scattered about the home: rainhats, rainboots, fisherman's pants, etc. She was prepared for a life filled with water, Lazy thought.

Pubah and Lazy had their hearts set on each other. They spent most of the day talking. They talked about each other's book collections. Lazy found books on Pubah's shelf that sounded as though they demanded great energy to read, let alone integrate into one's life: *The Homeowner's Guide to a Homeowner's Job, Fly-Tying Even You Can Do, Electricity Made Easy, Notes on Einstein, How to Build Furniture, Make a Kite that Flies, Why Not Go Solar Now?* and *Let's Dance*. This last book was quite small and had tiny footprints all the way through it.

Lazy told Pubah that the kind of books she had sitting on her shelves were different. "A lot of novels and short story collections. And a few books about symbols. You never know when you'll want to look up what something really means."

"Like what?" Pubah asked.

"Oh, like a circle, for example."

Pubah smiled, "But don't you have any how-to books?"

Lazy thought for a moment. "The only how-to book I have is *How to Train a Whippet*." She patted her lean dog, Carson, on the ribs. "But I've never read it because Carson has never needed the slightest bit of training."

Carson walked over to Pubah and jumped into her lap. "She's very, very bony, isn't she?" Pubah said.

"Racing dog," Lazy explained.

When they finished their library talk, Lazy sighed, "You sure can tell a lot about a person by what they read."

Pubah, pinned to the chair by the sharp-boned Carson, looked as though her fate were sealed. "Or don't read," she added.

Lazy, who liked to think of herself as a kind of displaced Midwestern Bohemian, did not always trust strangers. It amazed her that she had left the Midwest. It dumbfounded her that she had left her mother's womb. Yet she liked people, especially this Pubah.

"I like you," she said.

Pubah, who thought of herself as hearty and warm, responded, "Same here."

They thought of things to do together. "Let's go to the movies," Pubah suggested. They went to the movies. "Wasn't that stimulating?" Pubah asked outside of the theatre. Lazy agreed. She had been stimulated.

"Want to go camping?" Lazy asked shyly.

"Yes!" replied Pubah. Lazy nearly collapsed from the force of Pubah's enthusiasm.

They went camping. "So refreshing!" Pubah exclaimed, stalking through the forest. "Ever been to the ocean?"

Lazy had been to the ocean, but they went there too. As soon as they arrived, Pubah leaped out of the car and ran down the beach right into the water.

Then, "To the mountains!" Pubah commanded. Lazy began to notice that Pubah had a very big supply of energy. They found themselves on a mountain. "Let's make love," Pubah said quietly on the mountainside.

Lazy hesitated. "Wait a minute," she said. "What about my boyfriends?"

"What about them?" Pubah wondered, lying on the grass stretching her golden arms over her head. She yawned and wrapped her hands together at the back of her neck. "I promise I won't take any of them away from you."

"Well, this won't be easy, Pubah."

"Why not?"

"Well," Lazy sought the correct words by examining trees, shrubs, sky. "Because I'm a woman, you see. And so are you."

Pubah narrowed her eyes and looked distrustful. "You're kidding."

"About what?"

"I'm a woman? You're crazy."

Lazy was kind of mystified. "No," she said seriously, "I'm not kidding. I'm not crazy."

Pubah jumped up, ran to her backpack, and pulled out a small round mirror. She looked at her face. "Hey!" she shouted. "I am! I am a woman!" She turned around and beamed at Lazy, her brown eyes filled with admiration and love. "What a brilliant person you are, Lazy." She rushed to embrace her. "I'm so very happy I'm a woman. I've always wanted to be one. Wow. I'm thrilled."

"Pubah." Lazy was suspicious and trying hard to breathe within the intensity of the hug. "I think you knew that."

Pubah kissed her on the tip of her nose. "I tricked you," she admitted. "I had to," she insisted, "because I had to trick myself."

Lazy kissed her back. "Okay, we're tricked. But listen," she warned, "I'm not going to be anything but happy about this."

"Right," Pubah agreed.

Hey, I am a woman!

Remembering those times made Lazy smile. She took her feet out of the water and she and Carson went up the ramp to the woods to find flowers. They found lizards and snakes, mole holes and poison oak, piles of debris, an old boat adrift in a sea of ferns, a treehouse where someone had spent the winter in a rocking chair, a washing machine with its motor standing next to it, and the tracks of several strange animals.

It was not until Lazy heard the buzzing of some bees that she managed to sight a flower. Lazy was hardly a botanist. "Plant," she had stated flatly to the bewildered botany professor late in the term as she pointed to pictures of green growing things in her college textbook. On the next page were flowering things. "Flowers," she said, waving her hand at the photographed bouquet. Then she went to the window and looked outside at the scenic campus. "And trees! Isn't that all there is to it?" The professor had given her an F but she was not sure she cared because her mind was turned always to literature.

Now she wished she had paid more attention because she thought that some of the flowering things she saw might be weeds. She picked them anyway. They looked like daisies. She put them together with little purple bell-shaped buds and took them all back to the riverhouse, cut off the multitude of furry bottom parts and threw these into the river. She stuffed the flowers into a jar and waited for Pubah to come home.

Pubah was delighted by the flowers. "My romantic nature inexpensively fulfilled!" She had brought home a bottle of Dubonnet Blond. They opened the wine and all the doors and windows, put Van Morrison on the stereo and placed the bouquet in the center of the canoe. Then they paddled out under the stars. The music floated over the dark river and the night embraced them. They laughed.

Saving the World
◆ ◆ ◆

Pubah had second thoughts about going to China.

"I have a lot to do right here in these United States," she said one morning when she was reading the newspaper. From time to time she would cover her face with both hands and make a sort of cry. Then she would say, "Listen to this," and read something awful. She liked to read awful things about energy. "Another 24 million dollars to repair a nuclear power plant. Great!" Or, "I can't stand it, people are spending $200 to $300 a month to heat their houses!"

These horrors built upon each other until she was led to conclude, "I had better start my inventions."

"Like what?" Lazy asked.

"Well," Pubah thought for a minute, "just about everything is needed as far as I can tell. One thing I can see is needed right away is some kind of massive energy field . . ." she pondered, ". . . maybe in the desert . . . solar reflectors, pipes . . . ."

Lazy was lost. She was not very good at inventions or imagining what Pubah saw when she looked off into the distance, as she was doing. The best she could come up with was an image of the most primitive sorts of mirrors with pipes leading from them to peoples' homes. "Will that work?" she asked.

"Oh, sure it will," asserted Pubah who began making drawings on a napkin.

Lazy looked on with respect.

"I'm going to invent a lot of electrical and solar things to save the world. I'll do it in my spare time," Pubah told her.

Outside their window, slow white sails billowed in a southern wind. Puffs of white from cottonwood trees filled the sky with cotton snow. Lazy loved and admired the world.

"Thanks," she said.

Pubah's Favorite Foods
◆ ◆ ◆

What are your favorite foods?" Lazy asked Pubah one fall day, as if she hadn't noticed.

"Bananas and yogurt," Pubah said while slicing a banana into a creamy pile of honey yogurt. "The best."

"Didn't you just have a banana an hour ago?"

"Why, yes, and I plan to have another pretty soon."

Lazy had been studying diets. "Do you know that macrobiotics suggest eating only food that grows in your part of the world? Bananas don't grow in Oregon."

"They don't?"

"Absolutely not."

Pubah placed a full spoon of bananas and yogurt into her mouth. "Well, that's okay," she said through the thickness, "because Oregon isn't my part of the world."

"No?"

"No. I was born in Detroit. That's Michigan. Michigan is my state."

"Difficult is your state."

"That too," Pubah laughed.

"But what about roughage?" Lazy persisted. "All the books say you're supposed to have roughage."

"I have roughage," Pubah insisted. "I'm an electrician. You don't think it's rough carrying around tons of pipe all day and listening to off-color stories while you're trying to eat your lunch? It's rough, believe me."

"I give up."

"Here, have a bite."

Crowning Pubah
◆ ◆ ◆

J odie was visiting and had an idea. "When Pubah comes home, let's crown her queen. She's been working hard all day."

Lazy thought this was a good idea. "Pubah S. Queen," she tested the notion. "Sounds good."

"What's the S. for?"

"Her real name, of course."

"Oh," Jodie nodded. "What should we make the crown out of?"

Lazy found what she thought was decent crown material, Christmas paper of a metallic gold. "How about this?"

"Fine." Jodie went to work on the crown, talking the whole time. "Now listen, when Pubah comes home, when we hear her coming down the ramp, you get the crown ready . . ."

"Uh huh . . ." Lazy appreciated theatre.

". . . and when she comes in the door we say, surprise! And then you put the crown on her head—we'll have banners up and stuff—and you'll have dinner all prepared, or something really special, you know."

"I know exactly. Something special."

"Right. And then I'll hand her a note and the note says, 'Look in your saxophone case.' In her saxophone case will be another note and that one will say, 'Look on your artist easel.' Then, let me see . . ."

"Another one that says, 'Look behind the telescope,' " Lazy offered lazily from the couch.

"Perfect. That one will say, 'Look inside the Chinese trunk,' and that one will say, 'Look in the toolchest,' and in the toolchest will be the last note and it will say, 'We love you.' I did this once for my mother and the last note was in the oven. She liked the whole thing."

"Good recipe for something to do." Lazy admired Jodie's imagination.

"I have a lot of good ideas." Jodie smiled.

When Pubah came home and was crowned queen and searched out all of her notes, she graciously accepted both title and love. "Can't think of anyone more deserving," were her final words to her subjects on the subject.

They were gratified.

Childhood
◆ ◆ ◆

Pubah and Lazy were not expecting an ice storm but they had lived in Oregon long enough to know that, weatherwise, the Northwest had a license to carry on unpredictably. Late one night Lazy went out on the deck to pick up another log for the fire and saw that the ramp leading to land was covered with a sheet of ice. She came into the riverhouse in an agitated state.

"We're trapped!" she told Pubah. "Land is no longer available to us."

Pubah was reading Barbara McClintock and wondering how she herself would redesign humanity. She looked up at Lazy. "What do you mean?"

"Ice." Lazy hugged herself inside the goosedown jacket she was wearing. "The ramp is frozen over with ice. If we try to go up that ramp we'll slide around like those little beads in a hand-held pinball game."

Pubah noticed that Lazy was actually pale and worried. "Come here." She patted one of the soft cushions on the couch. "Come and sit next to me and I'll find something for us to do so that we don't have to think about the ice. Ice melts, you know. Eventually."

Lazy was still thinking about it. "That ramp is so slippery we'd be in the river in a second. Soon as we tried to climb it. We'd freeze to death in that water."

"I have just the thing to take your mind off this ice storm, Lazy."

Pubah got up and came back with a shoebox that she had kept for a long time under the bed. She blew off a thin coating of dust.

"What's that?" Lazy looked up from her fascination with death.

"It's my childhood," Pubah said. "I don't show it to everyone."

The box was full of sketchbooks, crayon drawings, first grade mimeos with *T* words and *S* words. It held old photographs in which Pubah, looking much the same, grinned out at a world just waiting for someone like her.

There were many drawings of a clubhouse, sometimes in a tree, sometimes on land. "My brother Jimmy and I had a club," Pubah explained. "We were the Atoms."

Sure enough, there was a yellowed copy of a membership card:

I, Pubah *promise to obey the laws of the Atoms for as long as I will
be in it. If I quit I promise not to give out any information AT*

ALL. *During the clubhouse meetings I will not:* GOOFOFF, MAKE UNWANTED JOKES OR ANYTHING THAT WOULD DISTURB THE MEETING.

Then it said: *THIS I SWEAR BEFORE GOD*.

"Did you belong to a club, Lazy?"

Lazy shook her head. "I don't remember belonging to a club with a name and a membership card. Back in the Midwest there were the FHA and the FFA, but I didn't belong. The FFA was Future Farmers of America and the FHA was Future Homemakers of America. They kind of went together."

Pubah took out some drawings with writing on them. "Here are some of our trap cards." She handed Lazy two cards drawn in pencil.

There was also a short story about something called a Blood Freach. "Cross between lamprey and leach," according to the young Pubah's notes.

Pubah stretched her legs toward the fire and reminisced. "My most admired person in childhood was my mother. I loved being around her. Once I even took her on a wild goose chase. Did I ever tell you about that?"

Lazy shook her head as she crawled out from her big jacket and settled into the warmth of the fire.

"Well," Pubah began her story, "in my neighborhood in Detroit there was one place we were not to go. The Swamp."

Lazy nodded, although it was difficult to picture a swamp in a city like Detroit. She was just verging on thoughts of crocodiles when Pubah stopped her.

"Well, it wasn't really a swamp, but we called it that and naturally we went there all the time. It was a grassy place with a little lake and deep kind of watery mushy areas. Once I wanted so much to be with my mom that I came rushing into the house and told her that I knew where my brother Jimmy's missing bike was. It was in The Swamp. It had been missing for over a month."

"Was it in the swamp?" Lazy wondered.

"No, it wasn't, but I hoped she would come with me to The Swamp because it would be so much fun to be with her. So we got onto another bike, my bike. I got on the back and she got onto the seat and off we went down the hill and through the woods toward The Swamp. The wind was blowing her hair and my hair . . ." Pubah waved her hands around her head like the wind, "and I was really happy and then my mom said over her shoulder—'This had better not be a Wild Goose Chase.' I had no idea what a Wild Goose Chase was, but I had a horrible feeling that was what we were on."

"Oh my goodness. What happened?"

"Well, we got there, the missing bike wasn't there, of course, and so we went on home and I learned what a Wild Goose Chase was, and I also learned that for the first Wild Goose Chase one takes one's mother on, there is no punishment."

Pubah picked up the old photograph of herself and looked at Lazy with tears in her eyes. "My childhood's all gone," she said. "Wasn't I a sweet one?"

"You were." Lazy kissed Pubah's cheek. "You certainly were."

"What was your childhood like, Lazy?"

"It was especially good," Lazy considered, "because I had a Norwegian Aunt Meta who taught me to read, and I've always told stories. Before I could write them myself Aunt Meta wrote them down for me. Now of course I write them without that kind of assistance, as you know." She smiled an independent sort of smile. She went to her room and brought back a picture of herself standing next to a birdbath, holding a book. Her eyes were downcast.

"You look worried. Even then you were worried quite a bit, huh?"

"You never know what will happen. Of course if you did know that would be a whole other thing to worry about," Lazy sighed. "In my earliest moments on earth, though, I'm sure I didn't worry. I was right at home. I was small and the world was big and new and I liked it. I remember sitting outside my grandmother's house in North Dakota when a great hailstorm started and I was catching chunks of ice that fell out of the sky. They hit me on the head and melted in my hair and they melted quickly in my hands. Suddenly the storm was over and I sat down in the mud on the dirt road leading to Hawkin's farm. I was shaping the mud into big pies when, for no reason, I looked up and saw giant colors in the sky. I had no word for it. It was just Sky Full of Colors. I rushed into the old white house to get my grandmother. I thought those colors had never happened before and that she ought to see them. She came outside. 'Rainbow,' she told me and I thought that was a beautiful name. I was filled

'Rainbow', she told me...

with the smell of mud and wet grass. I was like a thing growing out of the earth and my grandmother was all in white. She had white hair and wore a white dress with little daisies on it—and a white apron. Her hands were powdered with flour from her baking. She smelled like woodfire and warm bread as I leaned against her looking into the colored sky. That was the first time I ever wanted to go up into the sky. I wanted to be a bird. Ice balls and rainbows! What a place the sky was! I thought it had a lot to offer."

"You weren't worried one bit."

"Nope. And sometimes even now I know there's nothing to worry about. Not really. I know I'm just molecules. Just water and earth and air and a spark of life. I'm just part of the whole thing."

Pubah put her arm around her and suddenly the fire cracked and Lazy remembered. "But sometimes," she said, listening to the wind and the hard-driving icy rain, "sometimes this earth is a little treacherous for my tastes. You know, Pubah, we would tumble down that ramp like nickels tumble out of a slot machine and land *plop!* right in the freezing water."

Pubah held her more tightly. "Let's just not think about that ramp or going anywhere. Let's just sit here in front of our warm fire and be like kids off in our own little house on a river in the Oregon woods."

Lazy looked skeptical but comfortable. "Life is dangerous, Pubah."

"Yes, it is, but only sometimes. Just remember Aunt Meta reading you stories and listening to the stories you told. Remember your grandmother in the kitchen making cinnamon rolls and the house all warm and cozy and all the love in the world around you."

"All the love in the entire world?"

"Everybody, everything . . . loving you."

Lazy mumbled, "We'd slide down that ramp like . . ."

"Shh." Pubah lowered the light in the kerosene lantern. They looked out the big window at the darkness around them. Lazy noticed that in the moonlight the iced rain sparkled as it hit the water.

Love
◆ ◆ ◆

L azy loved Pubah and loved loving her. Out past the edges of the world's agreement, beyond even her own standards, her own approval, the rules of her childhood, beyond even her own mind, she loved her and loved loving her. The loving brought forth in her all of her courage as well as all of her limitations, all of her blind desire to be like the others, to melt in, to be invisible. It took her out of the roles she thought she would grow up to fill. It took her away from her automatic stream of pictures of what life should be and forced her to create her own version of what life could be. And beyond all of that was the woman she loved, living a life made from nothing more than her own imagination, and she was beautiful.

Lazy loved loving her, daily loved watching the transformation from construction worker to friend as the dust was showered away along with layers of frustration. Loved watching her wrap herself in silk, gold chains floating down to her breasts, hair smelling of lavender and rosemary and body creamed once more to softness. Out of this wonder, the laugh emerged again, soft at first, then deep and loud and affirming. Lazy loved loving her, loved holding her, loved holding one of life's originals in her arms.

A Trip to Seattle
◆ ◆ ◆

Lazy wanted to go to Seattle to visit Catlin and Al and Rosita. Elby said she was going to Seattle on business and why didn't Lazy come too? They said goodbye to Pubah and left in Elby's maroon car with the heater and the radio that worked, and drove northward into the rain. Soon they were chirping away about their favorite topics: books and the human mind.

Few friends talked with Lazy about books the way Elby did. Elby was the daughter of two authors and books had paid her way through college so she had an above average interest in them. First they discussed some books they had read recently.

"That was fascinating about Colette's apartment, didn't you think?"

"What about that Mallory book—boring, boring, boring."

"Yeah, what was the point of that?"

"I laughed at that great description of PMS in . . ."

They talked on and on. Elby, ever the intellectual, moved the subject over to language itself. Lazy tried to keep up with the rapid-fire pace of Elby's brilliant mind.

"Novels really show how people are thinking these days. It's so interesting to think about how we use language, the language of books, the language of our daily lives. I've been wondering: What if most of life takes place in how we talk and how we listen?" They drove onward through the dense screen of rain to the precisely timed slap of windshield wipers.

Elby went on, "If you live in a world of objects," she speculated, "doesn't it seem that all you can do is shuffle around what's already there? But if you live as if the world is made out of—literally created out of—language, then you live in a world of possibility, a world of openings."

"Yes, indeed," Lazy agreed with her, thinking how good it was, especially for a writer, to think this way.

They drove on in their plush red nest, the bright green lights steady on the dashboard, the yellow lights of other cars streaking by, their voices full of curiosity about what really was or wasn't so about living. Lazy was happy in this little world with Elby. They understood each other.

As the hours passed they dropped philosophy and reminisced about the summer Lazy and Pubah had gone to Michigan to visit Elby and her parents in their cabin on a wooded island.

"My home state!" Pubah had repeated and repeated when she and Lazy got off the plane. They rented a car and entered the north woods. "There are bears up here," Pubah said to Lazy. "Look for them."

Lazy was dismayed at the thought of bears and tried to ignore this suggestion. When they got to the cabin, Elby and her parents were waiting for them. They all hugged and kissed and sat by the fire in the big high-ceilinged room. They drank wine and talked and talked. Elby's mother loved words and books. Her voice was like a waterfall, Lazy thought. One gorgeous phrase after another fell from her mouth. Elby's father looked like Hemingway in Bermuda shorts, plaid shirt, a full white beard, and cap. He chuckled and loved everybody and made puns.

After awhile Lazy noticed there were arrows shot into the wall above the fireplace and, sure enough, a bear skin hanging over them. She shivered.

"Are there really bears here," she asked, "or is that from Canada, maybe, or Illinois."

Elby's mother got very excited. "Yes, oh yes, there are bears here. They go foraging in the dump at night." Her eyes got big. "Let's go to the dump tomorrow night and see them."

This was not what Lazy had in mind.

"They only come at twilight," Elby's father said.

"I can't wait!" Pubah actually shook with excitement.

"Oh, Pubah!" Elby's mother beamed at her. "Such *joie de vivre!*"

So at twilight the next day everybody drove through the woodsy roads to the dump. When they arrived, to Lazy's astonishment, Elby, her parents, and Pubah all got out of the car.

"Where are you going?" Lazy tried to sound like a polite guest, but she actually shouted at them. It was bad enough to be in a smoking dump at twilight with bears expected, but to get out of the car and offer up an entire group as bear supper was unacceptable. Lazy stayed in the car and tried to meditate, preparing herself to see her beloved friends and Pubah disappear into the jaws of black bears, even now sneaking through the falling light.

Lazy looked at Elby's parents. "They may be intellectuals," she thought to herself, "but they need training in common sense."

Other Michigan islanders came to see the bears. They got out of their cars too.

Lazy unrolled her window a crack and heard the whole group talking excitedly about bears. "Yeah, we saw a couple here last night," the islander said. He was wearing a cap covered with fish lures and buttons that demanded everybody do all kinds of things in snowmobiles.

"Lots of bears," his wife said. "They came just about this time. This is bear heaven, this dump."

Quickly Lazy rolled her window up again.

Everybody waited and waited but no bears came. The islanders left and finally, in the pitch blackness of night, Pubah and Elby and Elby's parents all climbed back into the car. They were all grumbling and apologizing except for Elby's father who winked at Lazy in the rear view mirror. "Barely escaped, didn't we?"

Lazy was ecstatic but determined not to insult her hosts. "No bears!" she screamed with delicious relief inside the privacy of her own head all the way back to the cabin. "Yea! Yea! No bears. We're saved to live another day."

Elby laughed as she drove along the road to Seattle, remembering Lazy's fear of bears.

"Elby, a person ought to be afraid of some animals. I don't think bears should be harmed or anything—ever. They're associated with the goddess Diana and are therefore lunar creatures, but they are crude lunar creatures. They represent the baser instincts. And they probably get tired of smoked dump food, wouldn't you think? That means they could go after . . ."

In a few minutes Elby dropped Lazy off at Al's office. "I'll pick you up on Monday," she said, leaning over to kiss her cheek. Lazy went inside the office. Al managed a large brightly lit room of people who all hugged each other and worked on world transformation. That was their job. All the employees were leaving at the end of the day and Al came out to greet Lazy. They embraced and suddenly Rosita raced out from behind a curtain and grabbed Lazy's legs. She reached one small hand up. It was just barely big enough to hold a large green apple that looked as though it had been through the apple wars. The apple was bruised. It had been chomped on and was oozing.

"This apple is one hundred years old," Rosita said. "Eat it!"

"Never!" Lazy cried. She ran down the hall to hide. Rosita raced after her. Lazy ran into Catlin's arms just as Catlin, twinkly-eyed as ever, got off the elevator. "Lazy, you're here," she whispered. They hugged one another. "You've forgiven us. You've come to visit."

Rosita now grabbed all the adult legs she could and held on.

"I'm here to take you back to Oregon," Lazy said into Catlin's dark shining hair as she held her. "Oregon misses you too much."

"We'll take you home and make you supper, won't we, Rosita? Tell Daddy we're coming to get him. He's going to make us our favorite vegetable dish."

"Okay." Rosita flew down the hallway and Catlin and Lazy walked slowly arm in arm toward Al's office.

"So glad you're here," Catlin rested her head on Lazy's shoulder.

"Thanks." Lazy sniffled and reached into her coat pocket to get a handkerchief to dry her eyes. Intead she pulled out the big, oozing, child-abused apple.

"Yuk!" Catlin looked at the apple. "I hope that's not your idea of a gift to the hostess."

"Yes, here," Lazy offered the apple to her. "Eat this."

Rosita stood laughing in the doorway ahead of them. Lazy felt completely satisfied. It was worth it after all to leave her home, Pubah, and her pets just to see Rosita's delight and the feigned disgust and horror in Catlin's lovely eyes.

"Okay," Catlin said and grabbed the apple. "After all, you drove all the way from Oregon to see us. It's the least I can do." She opened her mouth wide to take a bite. Al appeared behind Rosita, saw her, and came running. "Catlin, no! Don't!" He grabbed the apple and examined it.

"Oh." He looked out of the corner of his eye at Rosita. "What a relief. I thought for a second this was a bad apple. Here, Catlin, go ahead. You have that for dinner and we'll have squash."

Rosita put her hands on her hips. "Stop! That's my apple."

The grown-ups swept Rosita into their arms and walked with her to the elevator.

"Your apple?" Al said. "Excuse me, had I only known . . . ."

When they got on the elevator and the doors closed and they descended to the street, Lazy gave a little prayer of thanks to gravity itself for bringing her to earth and to friends like these, no matter where they lived.

Jodie's Poems

◆ ◆ ◆

L azy's godchild Jodie sat quietly with a pen in her hand. "I'm going to write some poems about my favorite things," she said quietly to Lazy. "God, life, and ice skating."
"Take it away," Lazy told her.

The first poem was called *God*:

>God
>You helped
>me to
>be hear
>You helped
>the moonlight
>shine threw
>my bedroom window
>Thank you
>for helping
>all the
>wonderful people
>get on this
>earth
>especially
>LAZY LA RUE

The second poem was called *Life*:

Life
there are so
many wonderful
things to see
in life
but you usually
don't see all of them
There are so
many hard things to take
but some of them
aren't so hard
!
So when you
think you've herd it all
just remember there's alot
yet to come

And the last poem dealt with Jodie's favorite pastime, *Iceskating*:

The ice is chilling the
sounds they echo
The people stop
to watch her
then they wisper
"Wow she's good!"
The smell is of
sweet cherry
but when your
off the chilling ice your
sole is so plain
You say to yourself
the excitement is
gone the freedom
is gone but you get
back on it's a
whole new thing

   Jodie Slattery
   Age 10

The Problem Cat
◆ ◆ ◆

Carson was a mannerly whippet, an older dog who liked to take long naps and dream about things so interesting that her feet and nose twitched. Magic, black, sleek, and elegant, sat in the window and watched ducks most of the day. Max, a stray cat that came to Elby's doorstep and which she gave to Pubah and Lazy, was a problem.

Max was mostly white with the black and gray splashes of a tiger ancestor on his back and face. He had a short Manx tail, blue-green eyes, and a pink nose. His walk indicated he was proud to be incarnate in the flesh and fur of a cat, but he had no manners.

One day their neighbor, Jerry, met Lazy on the ramp and said, "You know I was fishing the other day and that Max . . ." Lazy put on her composed, concerned owner look when any story started with the phrase, "That Max . . ."

"Yes?"

"That Max was hanging around but I didn't think much of it. I had a little fish I was using as bait and put it out in the water and Max was sitting on a log, saw it flopping, took it right out of the water and ran away."

"Goodness," Lazy said, hoping to convey sympathy, "how rude!"

Max not only stole fish from fishing poles, but from fishermen's baskets, and he stole pork chops from frying pans, chicken from barbecues, and catfood from other cats. His favorite trick with other cats, in fact, was to lurk under the ramp like a troll and wait for them to pass over him on their way to use the forest restroom. Then he would jump out, arch his back, spit and cry and put up his dukes at them until, intimidated, they ran home and went to the bathroom elsewhere.

He often sat on logs and did his fishing for himself. Sometimes Lazy saw him sitting quietly on the big log tied to their house and suddenly one of his white paws would shoot into the water and grab a fish. Invariably, he put it in his mouth and came into the riverhouse to present it to her. One day he came home gingerly holding the head of a frog in his mouth while the frog's feet waved frantically in all directions.

Lazy always saved the aquatic life by combining lavish praise with the skillful removal of prey from tiny white teeth. Even though she threw it

The frog's feet waved frantically

back into the river, Max looked content and curled up to take a nap to rest from his exertion. He didn't seem to mind that he didn't get to keep anything from the water although he had different standards about small land creatures. These he hid from her and enjoyed privately, bringing only the remains for her to view.

Sometimes in the winter his fishing nearly killed him. He did not stop going out on logs just because the temperature dropped, and from time to time his paw wasn't fast enough and he toppled forward into the water. Then he came in soaking and shivering and Lazy had to dry him with a towel and hairdryer while he yowled and complained. He then demanded a special dinner to compensate for his near suicide.

His other favorite winter trick was to drop in anywhere, at anyone's house, when it got too cold to stay outside. Jo Anne might call early in the morning to complain, "That Max came into our laundry room last night all wet and muddy and slept on Charley's clean shirts!"

"Max, you're a problem," Lazy told him after receiving calls like the one from Jo Anne.

Whenever Max heard this tone coming from Lazy he immediately fell over on one side, revealing his soft white belly, and blinked at her with his big blue-green eyes.

"What am I going to do with you?"

At this tone he rolled onto his back and curled his paws at her in a most fetching way.

"Everybody complains!"

Now he flopped over on his other side and his eyes glanced around the room for something to play with, a lost coin, a dustball, a small piece of wood. Lazy adored him as he chased whatever it was around the room, sliding across the wood floor, tumbling over and over and over on his back, tossing the object into the air, arching his back in fake fear and shock when it landed, spinning around and around, batting the thing until, without fail, he stopped suddenly and walked with his little tail straight up over to the scratching post, and not the couch, to sharpen his claws.

"But what can I do?" Lazy lamented at this point. She sat on the couch and shook her head at him. This was his signal to climb onto her lap, touch her warm nose with his cool pink nose, purr and curl up to sleep. She was trapped by love until he awoke and she could get up and move around her home again.

Balloons
◆ ◆ ◆

Lazy had a lifelong question: How can I get around with the least expenditure of energy?

She liked to walk. That was easy once she was on her way, but when she was lying down it was mighty difficult to get up and go walking. Even when she was sitting, the thought of standing almost depressed her. Standing, she had to move and, moving, she had to get somewhere. Once there, something probably had to be done and, since she was there, she was no doubt the girl to do it.

This was a big problem when it came to the idea of travel because it was this same person who wanted to see the world and yet not go to a lot of trouble about it.

Planes were all right, but airports exhausted her. Also, once she got to an airport, she would often realize how far she was from home and her pets and wanted to turn right around and go back. Driving was trouble, trouble, trouble. One had to stay conscious, keep shifting gears, make decisions about stopping to eat, etc.

Trains were out of the question. They were too slow. By the time she realized she wanted to turn back on a train, the thought of riding one all the way back home again was unbearable.

Still, there was a world to see and now and then Pubah threatened to see it, so sooner or later, Lazy would have to find her ideal way to travel.

One day she saw a postage stamp that changed her life. On the stamp was a picture of a balloon called *Intrepid*.

"That's it!"

She began to dream of ballooning. All you had to do in a balloon was go up and come down. You could come down close to where you went up. You could take cream cheese and bagels with you if you wanted. You could decorate one of those wicker baskets with pictures of your friends and ancestors and drift around the sky completely safe and cozy. Lazy longed to look down on the forests and her river from a balloon. Sometimes, during naps or at night, she felt herself leave her body and rise upward, straight toward the clouds. *Intrepid*.

Ballooning, she decided, was a lazy woman's ideal way to travel.

One day Lazy discovered a book at a garage sale. She could not understand how someone was giving it up. The title was *A Romantic Look at*

Modern Exploration with Descriptions of Odd Customs, Titillating Adventures and Thrilling Discoveries of Explorers in All Parts of the World. It was published in 1906. The author's name was Henri Sylvester. The book had on its cover a picture of a camel and a woman. The camel was piled high with a small house that was covered with colorful hanging cloths. In front of the camel a woman, who wore a long dress that started at the top of her head and flowed to the earth, held one hand at her waist and the other at her side, a posture which seemed most definitely to suggest adventuring. A scroll in the upper left-hand corner of the picture described her as a "Traveling Tawarek Lady." On the spine of the book rose a golden balloon with an elaborate basket attached below it, and below that a polar bear stood against a red sun rising over ice floes. It had 26 illustrations. She showed it to Pubah.

"As a Sagittarian," Lazy explained, "it's natural for me to read about this sort of thing, if not do it. Sagittarians are great adventurers."

Pubah had no fears that Lazy was a great adventurer. "Read ahead," she said, "I've got my own reading to do." She patted a stack of magazines called *High Technology* and *Sundance*. "As a Leo, it's my task to know all about high tech and solar things."

Lazy looked at the cover of the book and talked on. "This balloon here appeals to my romantic nature and the bear, of course, appeals to my love of animals."

"Traveling Tawarek Lady"

Pubah was no longer listening. Lazy skimmed through the chapter titles aloud:

"Bandits in Iceland"

"Snowshoeing through South America"

"Embittered in Tibet"

"Noah's Ark in Norway?"

"From Mongolia to Chicago to the Pamirs"

"Kuwait Revisited"

"Surprises in Ireland"

"Ballooning to the North Pole"

She paused. "This is it." She turned to page 246. The story was a sad one. Some Scandinavians ("Our ancestors," she said to Pubah, "on my mother's and your father's side") were going to be heroes. Off they went in a well-fitted balloon to see the North Pole, never to be heard from again. At least not heard from by 1906.

"Nowadays we have very modern, very safe balloons, isn't that right?"

Pubah hesitated. "Well . . ."

"You know if I went in a balloon," Lazy shivered, "I would not go toward the North Pole."

"No, I can't imagine that you would."

"No, indeed. I would go over our river."

"Sounds good." Pubah began to read again.

Lazy continued. "Those guys had blankets, food, sleds, carrier pigeons, a boat . . . I'd take all of that plus Medaglia D'Oro coffee and my teapot, a bunsen burner, pictures of my grandmothers . . ."

Pubah looked up. "You don't really need all of that. These days you can go up and down in a balloon in one afternoon."

"Oh! Up and down. An afternoon."

Pubah didn't like the way Lazy looked as though she were really thinking about it. Lazy noticed. "You come too."

"No heights for me, thanks," Pubah told her. "My adventures are across land and ocean. I don't go in balloons."

"Up and down in one day. Just up, look at the river, then down, home for dinner." Lazy acted all of this out with her hand as a balloon. Pubah watched the hand.

"I'm not sure it's safe, Lazy. Those guys didn't come back."

"No, they didn't, but that was long ago and they had big things in mind. Big adventures. Not small adventures. I just want to go up and come down, to drift over my homeland for an afternoon."

They both saw that this was unlike the rest of their relationship. Here was Lazy wanting an adventure and Pubah trying to stop her.

"This is a switch," one of them said.

"Yeah," agreed the other.

They looked into each other's eyes, then Lazy picked up the book. "Well, let's see what else we have here . . . Look, here's a chapter called 'A

Peep into the Real Lives of Women who Love Each Other' . . . ." She winked at Pubah, who smiled.

"No thanks. I think I'll just go on reading *High Technology*. There are a lot of new things in the world besides balloons. There are a lot of things I could have invented myself if I weren't working all day. Look at this. It says here that microchips are almost outdated. I've got to get on with my inventions. I've got to save the world, you know."

"Maybe you could invent something today," Lazy suggested.

"Yes, I might. Later on I'd like to get a group of people together and invent a band. Call a meeting, you know, and get that thing going. By the way, you're on piano and I'm on drums and sax."

"I have not played the piano for twenty years, Pubah."

"Practice!"

Lazy smiled and closed her eyes. She leaned back in her chair. A bit of time in a balloon, she thought, would make a day quite fun.

Kalin and Suzana and the Ouija Board
◆ ◆ ◆

K alin and Suzana and Lazy and Pubah were very good friends. Kalin and Lazy were the original friends of the foursome. When they first met some years before at a YWCA, Kalin had worn her hair bleached blonde and flattened with a pastel headband that matched whatever New England print dress she wore. In those days she carried a basket for a purse that had a needlework cover which read: "Blondes *do* have more fun," and was engaged to someone who wanted to be a minister and did not recognize her aspirations to be the same, although hers were a secret perhaps even from Kalin herself. Needless to say, their relationship did not last.

For the first several years of their friendship, Lazy noticed that Kalin seemed interested primarily in folk songs and decoupage. When she heard about the liberation of women, Kalin said, "Oh, pooh," but soon Lazy was amazed to see her off to her first women's liberation conference in Chicago. For this event Kalin purchased new jeans, a new blue workshirt and a new red bandana which she tied over her very blonde hair. "How do I look?" she asked, ready for anything that could happen in 1969.

In modern times Kalin kept her hair its true color, a mainstream blonde, painted her fingernails, dressed fashionably, and was more like a priestess than a minister, or perhaps some combination of both. She both loved the divine and had a genuine interest in the occult.

Kalin shared a beach house with her friend Suzana. Suzana was a woodworker and painter. Hightower, their beach house, was crowded with Suzana's worktables and cabinets. On its walls hung canvasses covered with sand from the ocean, turbulent seascapes, and portraits of their many interesting friends.

"I'd like to do *your* portrait," Suzana said from time to time to either Pubah or Lazy. Suzana had such an unusual way with a brush it was a leap of faith, Lazy thought, to have her do your portrait.

On a cloudy afternoon Kalin and Suzana came to visit and brought with them a new instrument of occult communication. They put a flat package on the dining room table and, slowly, with ceremony, removed its silk wrapper.

Lazy and Pubah looked at the polished flat board. Befuddled, they

gazed at the brightly painted numbers and letters.

"It's a ouija board," Suzana cried out, unable to bear the suspense.

"Oh," they sighed together, "of course."

"But what does that mean exactly?" Pubah asked.

"And where did it come from?" Lazy wanted to know.

"That's the wonderful thing." Kalin's hand lightly touched the board, her painted fingernails resting here and there on a letter or number. "Suzana made it. I was doing some automatic writing, you see, and received an important message."

Suzana sat back in a chair, adjusted her glasses and assumed a modest look. Pubah and Lazy sat down and Kalin lit the kerosene lamp at the center of the table. They all felt a chill as the flame shot up into the darkening room.

"Automatic writing, did you say?" For as long as Lazy had known Kalin, and they were the oldest of friends, the woman was still a mystery to her. "And how does a person do such a thing as that?" She was wondering partly out of simple curiosity about the occult and partly because this automatic writing might be a method for writing novels that she had never heard of and that didn't involve much thinking or time spent. The word "automatic" combined with the word "writing" made her, in fact, a little dizzy with hope.

"To do automatic writing," Kalin explained, "you have to open yourself to spirits."

That sounded simple enough to Lazy. "And how does one contact spirits?"

A few drops of rain tapped the windows, the sky filled with dark clouds, and suddenly there was a storm. The roof of the riverhouse resounded with the downpour. Pubah put another log on the fire. Kalin folded her hands.

"It's pretty easy," she said. "You have to be open, that's all, and then of course you have to do what they say. For example, they told me how to get this board. The first thing they told me was to send Suzana to the logged land." She paused. "At midnight."

Pubah and Lazy gasped. "Not the logged land! Not at midnight!"

They knew that the logged land was a section of property Kalin and Suzana owned near the coast. The lumber people had gotten to it before their purchase and now, although it was re-seeded, growth was slow along the sad little stretch of graying cedar stumps. Thin twisted branches from felled trees littered the tall grass. On the stumps the rings that marked the lifelines of the old cedars were faded by rain and sun. Each trunk had been cut at approximately the same place and each juicy tree had been dragged off to the marketplace. It had been the scene of a slaughter and was now a graveyard with the new growth just barely visible.

"I didn't want to go," Suzana shivered. "Especially at midnight. But those spirits have a way of talking, right through Kalin's hand and pen. They wanted cedar and they wanted it now."

"For this very ouija board." Kalin tap, tap, tapped the board with her pointy red fingernail.

"I'm a good sport so I went," Suzana said. "There was no moon so I had to take a flashlight and creep around. I found the biggest pieces I could. The woods were growling with bears and coyotes and pumas . . ."

"Suzana!" Kalin poked her.

"They were!"

Lazy gripped Pubah's hands.

"So," Suzana went on, "I had to work fast. A week before one of our neighbors had seen Bigfoot lumbering along a forest path . . ."

Lazy felt an urge to sit on Pubah's lap.

Kalin chastised Suzana. "Look what you're doing. Poor Lazy."

Kalin recaptured the floor. "Anyway, the gathering of the wood, courageous though it was, was only the beginning. The spirits had instructions for the making of the board."

She pointed to the different aspects of the ouija board as she spoke. "It had to be polished and oiled and then all the letters of the alphabet painted in deep blue. Here they wanted the sun, here the moon, here a bright golden star, here the word 'Deliverance' in red letters, and here . . ." her hand shot across the board to the bottom, "here they wanted the words 'MOVE ON' in black letters."

"Tasteful," Lazy muttered.

"Very interesting," said Pubah, "but what should we do with it?"

"We can ask it something. Anything. I have this little planchette here." Kalin pulled out a cedar pointer with a small round window through which she could see the letters. She placed it on the board.

Lazy thought of a question. "Let's ask it what's in store for me as a writer."

"That's a good question." Everybody present had wondered this very thing.

"All right, ready then? Suzana, get a pencil and paper and write down the letters as I call them out."

Suzana did so as Kalin placed the planchette on the board and closed her eyes. "We are asking," she began in her even, steady voice, "what's in store for our Lazy, the writer . . ."

Suddenly the planchette whipped Kalin's hand around the board. She opened her eyes and shouted out letters that spelled nothing whatsoever as far as Lazy's quick mind could figure. To confuse matters the front door of the riverhouse suddenly blew open and the pounding rain doubled its assault on the roof. The cats ran under the couch.

Lazy was frightened. "Stop!"

Kalin removed the planchette from the board, breathing heavily. "Well, it's certainly never done that before. It was a powerful answer but unclear."

Suzana shook her head over what notations she had managed to make. "Nothing sensible here," she sighed.

"It seemed . . ." Kalin narrowed her eyes, thinking, ". . . it seemed to linger now and then at the spot on the board called Deliverance." She looked around at her friends. "I can't understand what these spirits mean by that, can you?" Pubah, Suzana, and Lazy looked just as perplexed as Kalin did.

"Let's just wonder what it means and not have to know right now, okay?" Pubah felt the mood ought to change because Lazy looked so concerned. "Let's play Scrabble, or start smoking cigarettes again."

"Powerful instrument, wouldn't you say?" Kalin winked at Lazy as she placed the board again in its silk wrapper.

Lazy was thinking about Deliverance. "Very."

Later when Suzana and Kalin left, Pubah and Lazy stood in the parking lot waving goodbye to them and Lazy wondered what it all meant. "What do you think about this business of automatic writing, Pubah? Do you think I could make something like *War and Peace* come out of it?"

Pubah shook her head. "I think what you have to write isn't one bit like *War and Peace*. I think the board was trying to tell you though to write a lot and write fast. It was just very excited about your writing, Lazy."

"And that business about Deliverance . . . what do you make of that?"

Pubah put her arm around Lazy's shoulder as they walked back down the ramp. "Deliverance is probably the name of your first novel."

Lazy felt suddenly very tired. "Let's take a little nap," she suggested.

"Good idea."

In the days that followed, Lazy didn't exactly forget about the ouija board's strange message but she didn't dwell on it either. She tried automatic writing once and got some kind of combination of the *Desiderata* and an unpleasant excerpt from a recent biography on Elvis Presley. Soon she drifted back to her normal ways, writing one word at a time and thinking out her ideas for herself. Now and then she looked up into the vast sky for some sign of Deliverance, but her mind couldn't hold the notion of it for long. Soon she became fascinated by clouds, the swoop of the heron, or the smoke that puffed occasionally from Mount St. Helens in the distance, and Deliverance, as was its way, eluded her.

Packrat
◆ ◆ ◆

One day Pubah decided to do spring cleaning.

"Time to get rid of the nonessentials," she told Lazy. "Here are my criteria: First, is it useful? Second, am I interested in this? If something does not meet these criteria to my satisfaction, out it goes."

Lazy had her doubts that anything was going anywhere. Ever since she had known Pubah, the woman collected. In the closet were snowshoes, backpacks, fishing rods, a banjo, a bag of fabric for a quilt, yarn, a puppet theatre, the Harvard Classics, several half-finished paintings, paints, brushes and stretched canvases, and a big Cotton Club box full of files. All were covered with dust.

To Lazy's astonishment Pubah began her spring cleaning right away. She took from the closet everything she did not use and determined who its new owner would be. "Suzana can use these canvases," she said, "and if I get interested in painting again, I'll stretch some more."

Soon she had every object ticketed with the name of the person it should go to. "You see?" she said, quite proud of herself. "It's easy. My life is going to be streamlined. It's spring doing this to me, Lazy. It just calls for it, just like in all the books and movies."

Next Pubah took out the Cotton Club box and Lazy went out to feed the ducks. When she returned, Pubah was dreaming over her files. She looked up at Lazy. "Gosh, here's my file on ball bearings," she said wistfully. "I started it when I got curious about how they made them so round and heavy. And look, here are my files on water rights and how to temper a cold chisel. Here's Soleri talking about the city, and this fat file is on metal identification. How can I let this one go, the dynamics of plant succession? Look at all these notes on landscape design, welding, the patterns in sheetmetal, building your own woodstove, the methods of manufacturing steel. Here's the map of my bike trip across Europe with Gaia's mom. The red x's are where we slept. We had a plastic tent and only spent fifteen dollars in Paris. Can you imagine? And here are my notes on matriarchal forms, the spiritual vs. the physical, the Achaeans, endangered species, hunger, hazardous waste, thermodynamics, year 'round gardening . . ."

"Pubah," Lazy interrupted her and noticed that when Pubah looked up her eyes were glazed, drunk on the accumulation of notes. "Now would be a good time to remember your criteria."

"Criteria?" Pubah lowered the file she was holding. "Oh, yeah, now what did I say?"

"Is it useful? Am I interested in this?"

"Well, of course I'm interested in all of it. Ball bearings, for example, didn't you always wonder . . . ?"

Lazy shook her head. "Never wondered."

"Well, suggest something," Pubah implored. "Look at these things, all handwritten."

"Maybe you could just tell yourself that you now know how to find things out when you need to. You don't need to have everything filed in a Cotton Club box."

"That's right," Pubah nodded. "Besides, once I write it all down, I know it anyhow. I really know this stuff." She tossed the files into a big paper bag. "Spring cleaning proceeds!" she exclaimed, and so it did.

The next day Lazy thought the houseboat felt lighter. There was a freshness to it and a sense of space that hadn't existed before. She found room in the closet to hang up some of the clothes she had kept folded on shelves so as to avoid having them pressed between backpacks and snowshoes. Pubah seemed lighter too.

"Glad I got that done," she told Lazy. "I wouldn't doubt that was laying some of the foundation for saving the world. The world needs to be lighter, have more space. I wouldn't doubt if the world is just overstuffed and that's probably part of the problem."

"Wouldn't doubt it," Lazy agreed.

Lazy's Government Job
◆ ◆ ◆

Overnight, the trees along the bank behind the riverhouse had greened. Overnight, a spider had spun her web above the threshold of the riverhouse so that Lazy, the first one out the door, emerged into the day with strands of silk in her freshly washed hair.

"Oh no!" she squealed, shaking and brushing at herself, "what if it's under my collar or in my hair?"

"I don't think it is," Pubah assured her.

Lazy would not be consoled. "What if it is, though? What if it's just waiting to crawl out this morning during my conference with that young polite CPA? There I'll be, seated across from him behind my government desk, sedate in my government clothes, solemn with my government purpose, and there she will be, a fat bushy river spider sitting on my shoulder, watching, as we talk about that tax credit."

Lazy's current job was to preside over a state tax credit in rather formal clothes. She had been hired on a short-term basis as a consultant.

Sleepily, Pubah brushed at the invisible spider. "I don't see it."

At the top of the ramp they turned around to see that the river and sky were one color, a whisper of gray. A salmon broke the water's surface, then quickly disappeared.

They turned toward the car again.

"What if he sees it?" Lazy was saying. Pubah shook her head. When Lazy wanted to worry there was no stopping her.

Combing her fingers through her thick dark hair, Lazy continued, "What if he tells somebody?"

In her office a half hour later, Lazy had forgotten all about the spider. She had dropped Pubah off at a construction site and was now wondering what she would do before the tax credit consumed her as it did every day, discussed, as it was, on thousands of sheets of paper and craved by so many, many people. She sat in her office chair facing the city as it grew pink with the rising sun. She looked upon churches, bank towers, and a park. The phone rang.

She answered, "Oregon Council of Economic Enhancement." She did not really know what this meant. Fortunately, her caller knew. He knew that this was the number to call for some relief regarding his taxes. She discouraged him. His work was repairing radiators.

"The repair of radiators does not encourage ancillary activities," Lazy disclosed.

He wanted to know what the hell that meant, so Lazy strived to explain, her mouth fluttering over words thick with financial and employment implications until finally she translated all of them into real language. They reached an understanding and he left her alone to face the opening of envelopes, files, and notebooks, all of which were filled, Lazy thought, with more than any human should have to know about any one single piece of legislation.

ORS 28.000 to 28.009. Suddenly, and without undue effort, Lazy was an expert on all the words found between these numbers and yet there were moments when she was thrown against it all by some question from a fellow in the office. She was hoping that wouldn't happen when a face peered in and queried her, "Would we need an administrative rule change to make this thing into an incentive instead of an after-the-fact windfall?"

She blurred and mumbled and called the woman to whom this tax credit once belonged. Perhaps she would know.

There was no answer.

"I'll find out. I'll let you know," Lazy assured the questioner.

The face withdrew.

She called the woman again. Not in. She considered ways to amuse herself and finally determined that the best way was to start a department newsletter in which all the people working in the office were compared to the breed of dog most appropriate. She decided to call it Dog News and send it out monthly to the staff. It would have a light touch and its goal could be to reveal the senselessness of inter-office fighting, one of the apparent by-products of economic enhancement. It could have the manager dogs relieve themselves near their office doors so that no one entered while they were out for a leisurely lunch. It could have an advice column in which basic relationship problems were solved by an unpretentious and insightful whippet.

Unpretentious and insightful whippet

When the woman did not answer for the third time, Lazy leaned back to write her a note over at the city bureau where she now worked. She put the file of a lead-recovery plant on her lap to hold her paper still and realized it was a file she had long been ignoring.

"Christine," she wrote, "where have you been? You do not answer your telephone and I have an important question about the administrative rule and another about a lead-recovery company. I hate to complain, by the way, but I am beginning to wonder, what have I come to?" In a few moments Lazy was writing on and on, mostly to herself. "Until I started this job," she wrote, "I had never given a second thought to pipefittings, terrazzo floors, shrimp canning, oxygen transport, destination reports, aluminum extrusions, poultry freezers, silicone wafers, or the manufacture of paint rollers. I reckon I lived in a sort of ignorant wilderness of the mind where all I cared about were Pubah and the canoe and the silent green fold of the river as the oar stroked her. What could I have done that would bring me to an exhaustive review of some stranger's devotion to the systematic recovery of lead from dead car batteries? I want to take some balloon trips, you know. I want to sit in the basket of a helium balloon and follow the river. Maybe Pubah will come with me. I want to write things too, but not administrative rule changes."

Lazy read the note, then dropped it into the wastebasket. The CPA didn't arrive and the spider didn't show its face. A man named Tony, who wore a tie covered with a flock of geese, came in late in the day and told her that the job for which she had been hired was almost complete and they sure had enjoyed her being there.

"I like your tie," she told him.

In the late afternoon, Pubah and Lazy drove home and talked about Lazy's short-term government job and said perhaps it was time for her to get back to her own writing. They returned to the river the same way they came. By dusk the water was as green as the hillside. They entered by canoe and passed silently to the post where the blue heron sat. While the moon climbed into the trees, they watched the clouds darken to purple and saw the ducks, in their holiness, walk on the water.

Whether or Not to Marry
♦ ♦ ♦

Elby married her lover. Pubah and Lazy attended the ceremony. Elby wore a white dress and there were flowers and candles. She had decided not to change her name.

"I'll always be Elby," she assured her friends.

At the back of the room someone sang music from an opera.

"Opera," whispered Pubah to Lazy, and took her hand.

The groom's ex-wife read a poem.

"Cozy group," Lazy noted into Pubah's dangling earring.

Absolutely everybody cried.

"Why are we crying?" Pubah wondered as they went out the door and down the street into the night when the ceremony was over. Lazy looked back. The night was starless, moonless. The small white church burned with a golden light inside. The arched doors were open wide, spilling gold and people into the darkness.

"Commitment makes us cry," Lazy told her. "We're so small next to commitment. When two people walk right up to it willingly . . ."

Pubah was picturing commitment as a dragon, then as the Loch Ness monster, so she was startled when Lazy said, "Shall we marry, Pubah?"

Pubah pictured them both in white dresses walking solemnly toward Loch Ness. She shook her head. "It's too frightening." Then, thinking the matter through, she added, "Actually, for us it would be both frightening and embarrassing."

"Well," Lazy tossed her head back at the church, "they were embarrassed and got married. It's not so fashionable to get married any more."

"According to the rules, they can."

Lazy had an idea. "We could get married and just invite our friends. No relatives or acquaintances. Then it won't be quite so embarrassing."

Pubah discouraged the notion. "How can we exclude anyone? They invite us to their weddings."

"How about some other kind of celebration then? Some ritual?" Lazy persisted. The night was cold and she shivered. She and Pubah put their arms around each other and continued to walk.

Pubah asked, "But what would it mean, Lazy, some ritual?"

"The same," Lazy kissed her.

"Then we might as well get married and we can't. It's illegal."

"How can that be?" Lazy thought of all the things that ought to be illegal and were not. "What about asking children to sit down all the time in school? That ought to be illegal and it isn't. What about wars, for heaven's sake?" And then, becoming more general and inspired, "What about history? History ought to be illegal and it isn't. We should abolish history."

"Lazy, history is legal and our getting married is not."

They walked close together through the woods near the church. The night talked along with them, using crickets and owls and the rustle of leaves in the wind for conversation.

Lazy had another idea. "Let's marry illegally."

"No."

"Why not?"

"What's the point? Legally means sanctioned, community support," Pubah reminded her.

Lazy considered. "Our community supports us."

"Yes."

"And?"

Pubah sighed. "It's not the same as everyone," she said, "everyone everyone everyone."

"I see," Lazy understood. "Not the same as everyone crying for it, wanting it to last and last."

"If it lasts, it's a statement," Pubah said.

"If it lasts, it's a joy," Lazy nuzzled her.

"For us."

"For everyone," Lazy said. "Joy to the world is joy to the world. Why is everybody so darned fussy about where the joy comes from?"

"I just want it to last," Pubah told her.

"Me too," Lazy nodded. "Forever." She paused. "Shall we marry then?" she asked.

"Too embarrassing," Pubah smiled in the darkness. Lazy could hardly see her.

They put their arms around each other. "Life's embarrassing, Pubah," Lazy said. "That's what the wise ones say. Shall we marry?"

PART II: HEAVEN AND EARTH

Permission From The Stars
◆ ◆ ◆

Kalin and Suzana's house, Hightower, was a haven for Pubah and Lazy. On the highway coming into the ocean village where their two friends lived, they felt themselves relax from the stresses of their daily lives as soon as they saw Suzana's signs. Suzana painted signs that told about everything that was available in the little village: wines, hotels, fine foods. All just ahead. Her signs hung above the local inn, the local bookstore, the local grocery, dentist's office, and realtor's. She had her own woodshop called "Coast Woodworker," where she carved and painted signs and made bureaus, desks, tables, or whatever took her fancy.

Suzana spent a lot of time in the woodshop knee deep in woodshavings while dusty photos of Georgia O'Keefe and Amelia Earhart looked on. She spent her time smoothing wood, sanding wood, and cutting wood with screaming machines while Kalin sat in Hightower a few blocks away with a ruler and colored pencils, ancient texts and maps of the universe, managing astrology.

One Sunday while Pubah sat in Suzana's woodshop with her talking about glueing, pounding, and manipulating wood, Lazy sat with Kalin and pored over her astrological chart.

"You have Jupiter and Uranus transiting your sun," Kalin explained to Lazy. "That could be making you a bit restless."

"Oh!" Lazy was relieved. "Jupiter is transiting Uranus. That's why."

"No, they're transiting your sun." Kalin had a hard time explaining astrology even to her best friends. No one else drew lines and aspects and tiny symbols all over large circles and no one talked about it much except her.

"Astrology is just a metaphor, Lazy," she said patiently.

"Like a poem!" Lazy knew literary talk when she heard it.

"Exactly! And then there's the fact that we're made of water, you know, and that means something about us and our relationship to the moon. Tides, you know and . . ."

Kalin could tell Lazy was not really interested in how it worked, only whether or not it had an answer for her. "And, anyway, what's on your mind?"

Lazy wanted to ask Kalin about the wisdom of an adventure in a balloon. "Given my natal chart, what do you have to say about my taking a little trip in a helium balloon? What do you think? Will I die from it?" she asked pointedly.

Kalin looked at Lazy's chart. "Sagittarius with a Gemini moon, Cancer rising, let me see . . ." she mumbled, "twelfth house moon conjunct Uranus . . . hmmm. *But* the sun is in the fifth house conjunct Mars. Well, I'll tell you what," she said, looking up from the chart, "I think if you go on a sunny day with very little wind you'll be fine. This Cancer rising here makes you want to stick close to home. That's how Cancer energy acts in a chart: Home, Mom, food, pets. On the other hand, this Sagittarius energy likes to roam. So if you could just roam in a home, so to speak . . ."

"I do plan to come right back," Lazy offered. "I won't be gone for more than an afternoon. And I can think of the balloon as my little home for an afternoon."

"Yes, do that. And remember you're a writer and that this whole trip has some purpose. When you come down you can write about it. With no purpose you might get a bit scared up there."

Lazy was grateful for this reading. She and Kalin drank some tea, then Lazy walked on the beach with Carson. "Now if I can just convince Pubah," she told her whippet friend, "I can rise and feel air as soft as angels' wings."

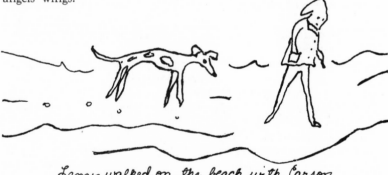

Lazy walked on the beach with Carson

Letting Go
◆ ◆ ◆

I want to go up in a balloon, Pubah."

"It is forbidden," declared Pubah.

Lazy looked out the window. *Intrepid,* she remembered. "I'm going," she asserted coolly.

"But why?"

"Don't whine, Pubah."

"All right, but just tell me why." Pubah was taking apart the clothes dryer so she could wash it with disinfectant. "I wish Max wouldn't bring his little friends home to play with and eat in the clothes dryer," she grumbled. "It's unnatural. Do you know what it's like to find mole parts . . ."

"Pubah," Lazy interrupted, "I am speaking of a topic which falls under the heading, 'romantic,' and I do not want to hear about mole parts at this moment."

"Well," Pubah looked up into Lazy's eyes and squinted, "tell me again, why do you want to go?"

"I want to see the rainforests from a balloon the color of Dubonnet Blond. Don't you think that sounds romantic?"

Pubah thought about it, then began again with the screwdriver and the clothes dryer. "I think it sounds silly."

Lazy continued, "I want to see our silver river from above, a necklace through the hundred shades of Oregon green. And eagles. And Annabel's pie shop on Sunset Highway . . ."

"You can't get any pies from that far up," Pubah said in a severe, practical tone of voice.

"I know that."

"What if the balloon goes pfffft?"

"It won't. You come too."

"Oh yeah," Pubah handed Lazy a handful of screws. "To repair it, I suppose."

"We can take pie with us."

"Pie at that height would make me sick. I don't even eat on airplanes. I don't like heights, Lazy. They remind me of construction."

Lazy could not imagine this. "I love to be high," she said.

"What if the balloon drifts off to Alaska?" Pubah wondered.

"Gold!" Lazy said.

"Job as a waitress, you mean, in some oilriggers' cafe."

"Money!" Lazy told her.

"You're optimistic. Oh yuk. Max! You cat! I hate this! Lazy, would you please get me some Pinesol, some ammonia, and some rubber gloves? This is surgery."

Lazy brought the required surgical materials. "I'd like to balloon over Doris Lessing's house," she said.

"My God, Lazy, that's in England."

"Well, Alusru Niugel's house then, that wonderful science fiction writer. She lives in Portland."

"Do we have face masks left over from the volcano?" Pubah wondered. "Because I need one now."

Lazy brought her a face mask, one of a dozen white masks that came in a volcano bargain package when Mt. St. Helens erupted.

"Listen, Laze," Pubah continued, "can't you just drive past Alusru Niugel's house? Look it up in the phone book."

"It's not the same!" insisted Lazy.

"Is this a Dorothy fixation?" Pubah wondered, strapping on the mask.

"I never liked Oz," Lazy said, turning her face away from the grim procedures and toward the river. "I'll do the disposing," she told Pubah. "Just tell me when you're ready."

"Yes, indeed."

"I tell you, Pubah, it's just the balloon I want."

"The balloon."

"Yeah," she said.

Pubah said, "It's time for the disposing person to take over her shift at the clothes dryer."

Lazy donned the rubber gloves.

"Well . . ." Pubah said, racing toward the shower.

Lazy followed her, "What does 'well' mean? What does it mean?"

"Well . . ." Pubah said again.

"I'm going!" Lazy shouted. "I'm going!"

"Would you please finish the clothes dryer job?"

"I'm going! I'm going!" Lazy jumped up and down.

Some crossbreed of cat and stone

"What if you don't come back?" Pubah called out from the shower. Lazy thought for a few seconds and then said, "Wait for me."

"Wait?"

"Yes. Invent things."

"I could get a lot done," Pubah said. "I could invent something to replace the common housecat for one thing. Some crossbreed of cat and stone that doesn't eat, that doesn't even think of eating, that doesn't even *remember* being predatory and that, if it remembered, wouldn't *dream* . . ."

"I'm going!" Lazy stared off over the river.

"Come back," Pubah called out to her.

"I will," Lazy promised.

Lazy Goes Skyward
♦ ♦ ♦

Pubah and Jodie waved at Lazy as she ascended in the golden balloon over the river.

"Gone!" Jodie shouted with excitement. "Gone to the sky!"

"Just what I was afraid of," Pubah said sadly. "Will she come back?"

"Oh, of course she will. Of course. I would have gone with her if my mom had let me."

Pubah was bewildered. "Oh, sure, why doesn't everybody go?"

"Now, now," Jodie consoled her.

"Is she really coming back?"

The balloon was nearly out of sight.

"She just wants to be gone for the afternoon, Pubah."

"Oh, no she doesn't. She wants to see Doris Lessing's house and that's in England."

"Who's Doris Lessing?"

"A writer."

"That Lazy does love writers, doesn't she?"

They shielded their eyes from the sun and looked into the expanse of sky until they could see the balloon no more.

Lazy, rising higher and higher into the brilliance of the day, became delirious with poetry. She took out her notebook and wrote:

"There are no bald heads on trees in July."

Then she reconsidered and diagnosed herself: "Altitude dementia." More hopefully she thought, "Maybe I'm too thrilled to write." Floating higher, she thought she felt the brush of angels' wings. Below, even birds in flight appeared to be nothing but dark shadows dotting the pale green earth.

"Africa!" she thought to herself. "I have to go over Africa next. Gazelles, elephants, lions, and giraffes. Or Japan . . ."

She looked down through the pure atmosphere and felt that she could grasp completely the mystery of the earth, the whole of it, its curve and soul, the much-discussed actual union of everything and everyone.

She thought of what Kalin said all the time: "As above, so below." She looked up, then down. Up, then down. Up, then down, and it was on this last downward look that she saw a new green, the blue-green of the

102

Pacific which was not on her itinerary. There below her was the stretch of beach where Kalin and Suzana lived, where she and Pubah and Carson had played a thousand times. Delighted, she floated past the great mountain Neahkahnie and saluted its eagle spirit. She drifted over the caves where the treasure from some sunken ship was supposedly buried, past the island with the lighthouse stiff and certain in the vast ocean. She bobbed down low enough to see whales on their slow journey and then ascended high enough to see ships as mere toys in the sea. And then, far beyond whales and ships and beaches, too high and too distant to see land or mountain or home, a moment came when, for the first time, a very simple thought occurred to her:

"Whoops."

A Message From Beyond
◆ ◆ ◆

Pubah noted that Lazy's balloon did not return by evening. "Well, that's wind for you," she shrugged. "Unpredictable." By the next morning Lazy had still not come drifting back so Pubah took out some charts and called the weather bureau. Together they tried to map Lazy's probable course through the sky. The weather bureau told her not to be concerned. "Concerned? Oh no, not me. Thanks very much."

But after another day of waiting and wondering, Pubah looked up from her electrical work and frowned at the blank blue sky over Oregon. "Where is she?"

She asked the same question of all their friends. "Well, she probably wasn't satisfied with just going over Alusru Niugel's house," Yancy suggested. "Maybe she floated down to California looking for more celebrities."

"I don't think so," Pubah said. She called the Coast Guard. "Send out an APB, please." They did so. Another day passed. No word. Pubah went to Kalin.

"How can I assist you?" Kalin asked when she saw her friend's sad face.

"Lazy's been gone too long," Pubah said. "Do you think the occult would have anything to say about it?"

"We can ask," Kalin offered. She took out her ouija board and she and Pubah sat in two overstuffed blue chairs. Pubah sat upright, very attentive, and Kalin commended her. "A straight spine helps the spirits come through. Now you write down whatever I say."

Kalin handed Pubah a pad and pencil and put the ouija board on her own lap. In an instant the pointer was flying over the board, stopping on this letter or that for milliseconds. "D," Kalin called out, then "O, U, B . . ."

Pubah wrote quickly. She was amazed at the speed of this form of communication, considering how difficult it must be for spirits to get their messages through the density of brain and bone and flesh and blood. "N," Kalin muttered, her eyes nearly closed, "O, T . . ."

Soon Pubah had a paragraph of words that ran together and sounded almost Biblical in their arrangement. "DOUBT NOT THE POWERS OF THE WINDS YOU CANNOT GOLDEN BALLOON KNOW

She took out her Ouija board

WHEREOF LIFE GOES ON INVENT LOVE IS ALL LOVE AND WORK SAVE WORLD."

Pubah looked at it. "It's kind of like a little telegram from outer space."

"Exactly," Kalin agreed. "And I think it means she's okay."

"What makes you think so?"

"It's just a feeling, Pubah. You stay busy and she'll come back. I just know it."

Pubah tried not to cry but she was concerned. "I want her back now."

Kalin began to cry. "I know."

"I'm already working hard, anyway," Pubah whimpered, defending her unique work ethic.

"But are you saving the world?"

"I want Lazy back."

"I think that's okay and you can save the world too. You and all the rest of us."

"Well," Pubah considered, "I have been meaning to do some more saving of the world. Just the other day I was thinking, 'now, why isn't there something we can just stand in to get clean that isn't water?' We waste so much water trying to get ourselves clean every day. I could invent something like that."

"That's a good idea."

"She could be back any minute," Pubah said, encouraged by her chat with Kalin.

"Maybe we should have a little ceremony to try to communicate with her," Kalin suggested, ever the minister.

"Ceremony?"

"Yes. We could talk about her and read one of her poems. You know how she's attracted to her own writing. Maybe that would bring her back."

"That's a good . . . that's a very good idea . . ." Pubah began but could not finish. Somehow she knew that she would work very hard at her inventions and that she would always love Lazy LaRue exactly as she did at this moment and there was nothing to do but work and love, just as the board said. But for now the loving meant she had to cry too. Soon she was sobbing in Kalin's arms and longing to be next to Lazy, for the touch of her friend's fingers entwined in her own and for Lazy's soft, slow voice to be whispering, "Happy, Darling?"

The Ceremony
◆ ◆ ◆

There was a ceremony at the ocean on the beach in front of the house where Kalin and Suzana lived. Kalin wore her priestess vestment, a long white dress and a colorful scarf with gold and silver threads. "Don't you think I look like an angel?" she asked Suzana. "Lazy would have wanted me to wear this."

The phrase of the day was, "Lazy would have wanted . . ."

Elby, Suzana, Jodie, Pubah, Gaia, Catlin, Al, Rosita, Wayne, Sarah, Sal, Dugan, Yancy and many, many others were there, an enormous crowd of friends. The sun was setting so of course the ocean looked like a million bucks, as though diamonds had been cast upon the waters and were sliding through waves of liquid pearl, just as Lazy would have wanted it.

Kalin asked everyone to make a circle of stones and they did. At its center, she placed a candle inside a deep crystal glass so that the wind could not blow it out. Then she asked everyone to say something personal about Lazy.

Kalin wore her priestess vestment

Pubah said, "Well, I don't want to because it sounds like she's not going to come back if we talk like that."

Kalin's voice was soft. "Say something anyway."

"I love her very much," Pubah said, and started to cry. Gaia took her hand.

"She always liked my paintings," Suzana said. "She had good taste."

Jodie called to the clouds, "You are the best godmother ever!"

Everyone voiced a little something on Lazy's behalf, even if it was only a plea to come back, then Kalin spoke. "I'm going to read a piece of Lazy's writing. Maybe the winds will carry her own voice out there to her and the voice itself will bring her back to us. And if not, well . . . she would have wanted me to read this."

Kalin read:

Now there are voices. What do you fear, they ask me. Make lists. Well, that I am not of this place, that I am not of it, that it is not me, that we are not made of the same stuff. My form is only seemingly its form and anyway all of this is a mystery to me and I never liked mysteries. And I fear the power of this place, the darknesses, the places where it seems to flow together whether I am there or not and oh, when bits of it break off and die and are gone then, and the wind. I fear the wind. Its raspy voice chills me, and since you ask I fear that there is meaning here and I'm blind to it; I fear there are tales to be told by all who live here and I won't understand what they mean. I fear my ignorance then, and the longing in me.

But I love brushing against it as I go by. I love the feel of it, making new shapes in it. I love the bird sounds and purrs and screeches and growls of it, and its texture. The spots that shine. The sparkles in the rock.

They all came together as Kalin lifted the glass high into the air in the direction where the balloon was last sighted. Then they left their circle of stones and went on home without her.

Newspaper Item
◆ ◆ ◆

L.◆ LaRue MacIntosh, mid-thirties, occupation writer/tax credit analyst, disappeared Tuesday in a Dubonnet Blond-colored helium balloon. MacIntosh was last seen heading west. Search parties in planes followed wind currents but reported seeing no sign of the balloon.

THE OREGONIAN

Inventions
◆ ◆ ◆

After the ceremony, Pubah went back to the riverhouse and made herself a workshop in the large spare room off the kitchen. She put bookshelves and her tools in it and covered the walls with sketches of things she thought could cut down on the world's use of energy. "Let the inventions begin!" she said to Magic, Max, and Carson.

In no time she was hard at it. By the end of the first day she had invented a hand-held instrument that sucked up and destroyed already-shed animal hair, and developed plans for making clothes that were self-cleaning, and automobile paint that would not oxidize.

Friends came by to see how she was doing. "How are you doing?" Sal called into the workroom the next day.

"Doing fine," Pubah called back.

Elby and Kalin and Yancy came by. "How are you doing, Pubah?" They gathered around her in the workroom and gazed upon the disarray of creation.

"I'm doing fine," Pubah told them.

Since Lazy had not drifted home as quickly as everyone hoped, they were glad to see Pubah so busy. In fact, Pubah was so busy she hardly noticed them. She liked inventing things and she liked the idea that her inventions might make a difference to the world. Not only did inventing keep her mind off Lazy's absence, but it was also a challenge bigger than most of her challenges, and she became obsessed with it.

"Want to go out to dinner?" Elby asked.

"I'm saving the world," Pubah told her. "Somebody's got to do it."

They agreed and left her alone.

A New Vision
◆ ◆ ◆

Lazy sailed through the bright sky comforted by the thought: "There are search parties out, by boat and by plane." She imagined a helicopter coming to save her. A young Coast Guardian would drop a line to her balloon and instruct her to loop it around herself. "Easy, Ma'am," the Coast Guardian would say. "There we go, that's it; everything's okay."

The only time she did not think this way was when she passed through a cloud. "I hope no airplanes come in here," she thought, then looked up at the bowl of fragile golden silk over her head. "Or large sharp-beaked birds." Passing out of a cloud she saw again the clear sky and her vast companion, the deep blue ocean below. In spite of her tendencies toward worry, this silent sweep through the majesty of sky over sea soothed her.

When the warm gentle wind arced through the silk and lowered her, she saw that the ocean was actually a blend of blues, greens, silvers, and greys, with white foam like horses' manes rolling through the colors. She inhaled the salty air and fell into a sense of wonder at the power and scale of life and, though lost, gave thanks that she, a tiny being in a tiny balloon, had been set free to see her planet from this vantage point on a rare sunny day somewhere along the Northwest Coast late in the twentieth century.

Below her she watched dolphins leap from the water to greet her. She called hellos back to them until she was hoarse. Then the wind raised her again. Once or twice she glimpsed a distant shoreline peeking over the water at her. Rising above the feathery clouds she felt like an awed and deeply grateful guest on the earth, just passing through. And she knew as she had never known before that, while she was here, the well-being of all the other guests and the mother/hostess earth itself, was in her hands, in her tiny hands, held in her tiny heart. As she drifted along, she no longer worried so much about herself and her own small death or life, but wondered what she could give toward saving this place for the whole of its natural life.

111

Deliverance
◆ ◆ ◆

L azy was glad for the bathroom accommodations fitted into her basket by Bob's Balloons in Scappoose, and glad too that she had brought along an abundant supply of dried apricots, almonds, tortilla chips, and mineral water. At the last moment she had tucked several contemporary novels and some copies of the *New York Times Book Review* into her pack, never imagining that she would actually read them. Now she tried out the pleasure of reading at such lofty heights.

The gentle southerly wind carried her and she read and thought about writing, saving the world, and her life. At the end of the day she put aside the books and stood up to stretch, then walked over to the edge of the basket and looked out at the sun setting over the pink and turquoise water. Below her a family of whales swam northward. She called to them, "Why don't more people write about you?" No answer.

She looked out over the calm water and wondered how she would write about the things in the books she had been reading. How would she write about relationships and places and ideas? What could she give with her writing that was new? Supposing her writing could contribute something toward saving the world?

When the sun disappeared Lazy curled up to sleep in a corner of the basket. Her mind was spinning in new directions with questions about writing. At first she could dream only of the questions themselves, then she fell more deeply into sleep and into dreams about Pubah and the riverhouse, her neighbors and friends. She dreamed about Max fishing on the logs, about Jodie in the canoe, about Pubah and her timekeeping notebook, and about Kalin and Suzana and their beach house. Toward dawn she had a long dream in which she was sitting on the deck of the riverhouse looking into the distance. Suddenly, on the horizon, a tiny boat came speeding in her direction.

"Pubah's solar-powered boat!" She recognized it immediately. What else could travel with such great speed and scarcely cause a wave?

"Lazy!"

"Pubah!"

The boat came swiftly down the channel and in a moment Pubah was alongside the deck. "Help me out of this thing, will you Lazy?"

In the dream, as Lazy reached out, she was an old, white-haired woman reaching out to an old, white-haired Pubah.

Pubah handed Lazy her thermos, a lifejacket, a lunchbox, and her saxophone, then raised herself up and climbed onto the deck. "I'm home at last!"

They held each other, then leaned back to look into one another's eyes.

"It's been a long time, hasn't it Lazy?"

They sat down on the deck holding hands. Pubah stretched her feet toward the cool water. "There's no place in the world like this one," she said.

"How was it out there in the world?"

"That world is in great shape" Pubah told her. "I wish you could have been with me. I hope you got a lot of writing done."

"Just this morning I finished a new book, *Caring for the Ancient Whippet*. But tell me, Pubah, did you find out what you wanted by visiting the world through its waterways?"

"I'm happy to report the world is working perfectly. It's like a little beehive out there, humming along as though everyone is using Elby's timekeeping system but without the notebook part. They're all managing themselves beautifully. A lot more people are living on houseboats. That's a step in the right direction. And hunger is ended and everybody is engaged in work that's satisfying to them. My inventions have helped cut the world's energy consumption in half and . . ." she sighed and put her head on Lazy's shoulder, ". . . and I'm glad to be with you again. I'm happy, though, that I saw in my own lifetime, late though it is in that lifetime, that the world is working quite well."

Pubah was thoughtful and quiet. Lazy listened as the river ran by. "But you know, Lazy, I don't really think my inventions saved the world."

"No? Did my writing save it then?"

"No." Pubah looked into Lazy's eyes and kissed the webs of fine lines at their corners. "I think we saved the world another way."

"How's that, Pubah?" Lazy looked into the face of her beloved friend and reached out to touch the fine white hair.

"Of course you had to write and I had to invent, but I think we saved the world by loving life, not by anything we did, just how we lived our lives."

"You're a very wise woman, Pubah . . . ."

Lazy stirred in her sleep. She opened her eyes and saw the stars floating over her, the dark night snug around her. In a flash she saw the whole dream again, saw Pubah's white hair, her lined face, the little boat, then it was gone. She wished she could reach out to touch Pubah, just to tell her she had had a special dream, but when she reached out, the loneliness was all she could feel. She drifted again into sleep.

In the morning when she awoke, Lazy remembered nothing of the dream or even of longing to tell Pubah all about it, but she was filled with the energy of her own life.

She paced back and forth in the basket. The wind carried her slowly through the wide blue sky and her thoughts opened up about writing, wider than any thoughts about writing had ever opened in her before.

She remembered Elby's conversations about language as possibly creating the world. "What if most of life takes place in how we talk and how we listen?" Elby had said. "If we lived as though the world were made of language and not objects, think of the possibilities. It would be a world of openings."

Lazy wondered: "If the world were made of language, what kind of world would I create?" She puzzled and wondered and munched on almonds and tortilla chips and drank mineral water and puzzled some more until, at sunset again, she remembered she was lost and alone. She longed for the river and her friends and Pubah.

"I'll write about them," she whispered to herself in a moment of inspiration. "I'll write about love and the river and trees and creation and Pubah and my friends." She became excited with the idea and wondered if the world could use any of what she had to say about all of that to save itself. "Well, what about fun?" she asked herself. "What about wonder? What about riverhouses, for heaven's sake? Where are the riverhouses in literature? What about ducks and muskrats? What about Pubah? Where, in all of literature, is Pubah?"

There was a shift in the wind but Lazy barely noticed it. She fell asleep with her notebook in her hand after jotting down ideas for stories about the river and Pubah and their love for each other. This time her sleep was deeper. She dreamed a vivid and exciting dream of mountains, volcanic eruptions, a triumphant Pubah and crowds of cheering people who seemed to be understanding something that had been puzzling. She knew she must remember this dream, but a rapid chopping sound and a very loud voice awakened her so abruptly that she flew from her unconscious without a moment's pause for remembering.

"Ma'am! Ma'am, wake up!"

Lazy looked up into the eyes of a young woman helicopter pilot. The woman was speaking to her through a megaphone. "Are you Lazy LaRue MacIntosh?" Lazy admitted that she was. "Then take this rope," the pilot called. "Hold on. I'm going to pull you over there and we'll land."

Lazy looked down. Miraculously she was over land again, wooded land, with a clearing almost directly below them that was big enough for a helicopter.

"Okay!" Lazy called, holding tight.

The helicopter moved slowly forward, then down. The balloon followed. They landed with a bounce in the clearing. The pilot jumped out and tied the balloon down, then reached up to help Lazy, whose legs were a little wobbly. Lazy climbed down from the basket. "Where am I?"

Juanita

"Just south of Coos Bay," the young woman said. "Coos Bay, Oregon. You'd better just go sit in the passenger seat. I'll attach your balloon to my chopper and then take you home."

"Home?" Lazy almost fainted with pleasure at the thought of home. "Yes, let's go there. I live on a riverhouse, just . . ."

"I think I know where it is. All of Oregon's been looking for you."

Lazy climbed into the helicopter and looked at all the controls. She sat very still so she wouldn't touch the wrong thing and shoot up into the sky again. Soon the pilot had the balloon tied on with a rope and some hooks so that when they took off, the balloon was suspended below them.

"When we get to your river I can let these hooks go and your basket will drop down on the water. Then you can just take a boat out to fetch it. I'll take you right to your ramp."

Lazy admired this person. "What's your name?"

"Juanita."

They shook hands. "Lazy," Lazy said. "MacIntosh."

"Yes," Juanita laughed. "I know."

Lazy leaned back in the passenger seat and closed her eyes. She felt the wind blow through her thick hair. Helicopters, she noted, traveled much faster than balloons. She thought about what a miracle it was that she would be delivered right to her own ramp. Then she remembered her question of Kalin's ouija board. "What's in store for me with regard to my writing?"

"Deliverance," the board had answered. Lazy felt calm and fully alive and full of her writing all at the same time. "Yes," she smiled to herself. "Deliverance."

Reunion
◆ ◆ ◆

Juanita radioed ahead so when she and Lazy dropped the balloon in the river they saw a crowd of friends and Pubah on the deck of the riverhouse. There were reporters too, with fancy cameras. Lazy liked all the to-do, but especially liked seeing Pubah again. When the helicopter landed, she and Pubah rushed to embrace each other.

Pubah was crying. "I thought I'd never see you again."

Lazy cried too. "I thought you'd be worried, and, you know, I had a wonderful time. I'm sorry you had to be afraid for me."

Then all the friends gathered around and the newspaper reporters asked questions like: "Did you think you were a goner, Miss MacIntosh?" And, "What do you have to say to your fellow Oregonians about their great state as seen from a balloon?"

"I plan to write to them about it," Lazy said. "Tell them they'll be hearing from me."

When the reporters finished taking pictures of Juanita and interviewing her, Lazy introduced the heroine to her friends. "Can you stay and celebrate with us?" Everybody applauded Juanita and thanked her for bringing Lazy home.

Juanita thanked them back and said she had to leave. "I have to go. You never know who else is out there in a balloon who might be happy to see a helicopter."

They all waved goodbye as the helicopter rose into the air. "There goes the chopper," Jodie said, waving at Juanita through the dusty air.

"I love that word, 'chopper,'" Lazy said, kissing Jodie on the forehead.

"Chopper, chopper," they said as they skipped down the ramp. "Chopper, chopper, saved by a chopper."

There was a big party and everyone swam in the river and played in the canoe and hugged Lazy as much as they could. All present thanked Kalin for her ceremony and for seeing the future so clearly that no one had worried all that much. Lazy hugged them all back and told them how much she loved them and after a while all the guests went home.

Pubah and Lazy collapsed on the futon to watch the sun go down. Pubah kissed Lazy on the tip of her nose. "You liked that trip, huh? Even though it was just about the worst thing that ever happened to me?"

"I liked it, Pubah. I liked it because not only was it so beautiful up there

116

... ever the vigilante against the Leo ego

that I almost crawled up onto the edge of the basket and leaped right into it . . ."

"That's comforting," Pubah nodded.

". . . but I also had a revelation about writing that will change my life."

"Oh? What's that?"

Lazy tried to think of how to say it, but all she could put into words was: "I know what I want to write about."

"Don't you always know what you want to write about?"

"Yes, Pubah, but I mean, I want to really write about this."

"What?"

"You."

"Me?" Pubah sat up, grinning. "That's a wonderful idea. You could write about me!"

"You Leos!" Lazy laughed and shook her head.

"Yes," Pubah went on. She looked with dreamy eyes up into the twilight. "That's a golden opportunity. You could call it *Stories About Pubah*, or *From Here to Pubah*, or how about *Gone With the Pubah?*"

"Do you think stories about you would appeal to anyone?"

"Everyone!" Pubah widened her brown eyes. "Don't you think everyone wonders about me and would like to know what I'm all about? How I'm wired together, what makes me tick, the Real Pubah?"

Lazy couldn't stand it. She began to tickle her. "Golden opportunity!"

"Golden yes," Pubah giggled. "Hey, stop that."

But Lazy, ever the vigilante against the Leo ego, could not stop herself. She continued to tickle in desperate defense of all the smaller egos in the world, the Sagittarians, the Virgos, the Piscean egos. Max and Magic and Carson, happy to have Lazy home, watched the humans roll all over the futon laughing and kissing and crying with love and happiness until finally, bored, the three animals wandered off in separate directions. The moon came up over the river, and Lazy and Pubah became quiet and let its light bathe them in their love.

117

Lazy Expresses Herself
◆ ◆ ◆

More than anything, Lazy wanted Pubah to go in the balloon with her. Every day she sat at her desk near the front window of the riverhouse and did her writing, but from time to time she looked out longingly at the golden balloon tethered to a float of logs on the opposite shore. Pubah spent much of her time now in her workroom, frantically inventing things to save the world. She did little else these days but invent and, to Lazy's way of thinking, she seemed to be in a panic about it.

Lazy had told Pubah about her incredible ride and Pubah was happy for her. "That's fine for you," she had said. "Now I can see you're the kind of person who needs to go up in a balloon occasionally."

"But what about you?" Lazy asked. "Don't you think a ride in a balloon would be fun? It's so exciting."

"Too busy," Pubah said the first time Lazy asked. The second time she said, "Too busy, and I'm afraid of heights, remember?"

"Heights, but Pubah if it weren't for heights, how would there be any perspective on this world? What kind of earth would we have with a ceiling 10 feet high? It's a blessing to be able to go up there. It's . . . it's practically holy."

Pubah only said, "You writers," and went on inventing.

Now Lazy sat in the window eyeing the balloon and wondering if she should just wait until Pubah went to sleep, then bundle her up, put her in the canoe, paddle over to the balloon, try to lift her into the basket . . .

The door to the workroom flew open. "Hey," Pubah called, "I have a couple of the best ideas for inventions that anybody ever had."

Lazy smiled at her. There was nothing quite as beautiful as Pubah in the throes of inventiveness. Her fine golden-red-brown hair created a halo around her face. Her eyes were as dark and shining as bowls of Colombian coffee. Lazy got a noticeable buzz just looking into those eyes at moments like this. "What's our heroine up to now?"

"Well!" Pubah paced back and forth. "I haven't got it all figured out yet, but I'm working on some kind of transformer for one's aura. When the weather gets cold, this transformer allows you to tune your electromagnetic field to a high temperature and you don't have to wear a lot of clothes to keep warm. Your aura keeps you warm. Pretty good, right?"

118

Her eyes were as dark and shining as bowls of Columbian coffee.

"Right."

"What are you working on, Lazy?" Pubah noticed the pile of papers on Lazy's desk.

Lazy patted the papers. "Oh, I've accomplished a few pieces of writing, as you see. I just finished a piece called *Spiderwebs: How to Learn Ecology Through Ordinary Things Around the Home.*"

"I thought you were going to write about me," Pubah reminded her, somewhat disappointed.

"Don't worry. You're in that story." Lazy picked up another stack of papers. "Here are a few notes for a little article I'm considering. It would be called *Pubah's Laugh: A Study in Breath Release.* And here," she picked up another pile of notes, "here are my notes on something called *Lazy and Pubah, A Twosome if Ever There Was One.*"

"Those sound fascinating." Pubah pulled Lazy closer. "What else?"

Lazy considered. "Don't you think there ought to be a book called *Lazy LaRue MacIntosh, Friend and Advisor to the Great Solar and Electrical Wizard, Pubah S. Queen?* Or what about an engrossing collection of stories about my childhood and everyday life called *Genius in My Own Right* by L.L. MacIntosh?" Lazy looked off into the distance, imagining these books, then she winked at Pubah.

"When can I see these writings, Lazy?"

"Oh, soon enough, soon enough." Lazy came back down to earth. "What else are you up to in your workroom?"

"I'm taking notes on an idea—and this one I also don't have all the details for yet, but I think it's a wonderful idea—it's a kind of transparent shield that you wear on your chest and when you're wearing it you will speak whatever is in your heart." She paused. "At all times. No matter what. Good idea, too, right?"

Lazy could see in her mind's eye a world of people who walked around speaking their hearts. "What if there are some emotions that should not be expressed, Pubah?"

"Of course there are powerful emotions, but what is there to hide, really? If everybody got to say how they were feeling, I'll bet ultimately we'd all be feeling love most of the time. That would be good to know and would feel good to express."

119

"I'm feeling something," Lazy remembered.

Pubah came and sat next to Lazy by the window. "What are you feeling, Laze? Tell me."

"Well . . ." Lazy turned toward the balloon then looked back at Pubah. If Pubah wanted everything out in the open, why not? "Well, I'm feeling sad that you won't go in the balloon with me. I've told you everything about how it changed my life and my writing and my whole . . . everything. And you're too busy or too scared to go. You care more for your time and your fears than you do about something incredible that I've done and want to share with you."

Pubah was silent. She looked into Lazy's eyes and saw the sadness.

"Lazy," she said. "I'm scared of heights."

"Yes, I know that. Trust me."

"And I am very, very, very, very busy."

"I know that, too," Lazy nodded.

"And . . ." Pubah began, and took a deep breath. It wasn't Lazy's sadness that she wanted to stop. The truth was there *was* something different about Lazy since she had gone off in that balloon. She was expanded somehow and productive and happier. Although Pubah had all of that in her own life, what could be wrong with having more? Life was risky, so why not choose the risk? She breathed out, ". . . I'll go." She heard herself say this and was astounded.

"What? You'll go? You'll go!" Lazy jumped up and clasped her hands together. "You'll go!"

"But only for a short trip," Pubah said, recalling her inventions. "I have to take my sax to get some practicing in and my notebooks so I can work on this auric field transformer and this heart thing and . . ."

"Take whatever you want, Pubah." Lazy hugged her. "Thanks so much for letting me give this gift to you. Thank you so very much. Your life won't be the same."

"If I have one," muttered Pubah as she trudged back to her workroom.

Heaven and Earth
♦ ♦ ♦

The next morning Pubah and Lazy got into the canoe and paddled over to the balloon. Pubah had her saxophone with her and some books with titles such as *You and Your Heart Chakra*, *Heartspeak*, and *What is an Aura Anyway?*.
"I plan to read these," she warned Lazy.

Lazy, who knew the domain of reality they were about to enter, only smiled. "Whatever."

Pubah didn't know what to think. Lazy seemed pretty certain about this balloon thing. They tied the canoe to a hook on one of the logs, got out and climbed into the basket of the balloon. Pubah looked up at the wide, empty blue sky. "Remember, Lazy, you got lost in this thing."

"Yes, but I've purchased and have been reading my book on balloon management." Lazy pulled the book out from her pack. "And see? I brought it along. We won't get lost."

"Better not prick this thing with a pin." Pubah pointed up at the billowing silk.

"Okay, I won't."

Pubah started to whine. "I wish all our friends were here to say goodbye." Pubah could suddenly think only of how upset she was when Lazy had disappeared and how frightening the whole thing had been. But all she could say was, "This is crazy. I have work to do!"

Lazy patted the cover of the book. "Balloon management," she repeated. Then she put her arms around Pubah. "It's heaven up there, Pubah, and well, you don't have to go. I'd be disappointed, but I'd get over it. Want to go home?"

Pubah thought for a minute. "Home? No, I'm an adventurer, too. And besides, I said I'd go and I'm going. My word's good on this river."

Lazy laughed and let go of Pubah. She began to loosen the ropes of the balloon while Pubah unpacked her saxophone from its case and sat on the floor of the basket to put it together.

Pubah could feel the balloon ascending, but she didn't want to look. She put the sax in her mouth and began to play. She played "In the Gloaming" and "Red River Valley" and was halfway into "Girl from Ipanema" when she noticed that Lazy stood at the edge of the basket with tears in her eyes. She was looking down.

"Lazy, what is it?"

Lazy shook her head.

"Lazy, why are you crying?"

Lazy seemed unable to answer.

"Oh for heaven's sake." Pubah put her saxophone down and stood up. The balloon was still rising. She walked over to Lazy. "I demand to know why you are crying."

But Lazy still did not speak. She only pointed, and when Pubah looked where she was pointing, down at the earth, she stopped talking too. She had only seen the earth from inside the plastic and steel compartments of airplanes, through thick tiny windows. Now she saw their strand of river joining with the wide silver ribbon of the Columbia. Spreading outward from the rivers were the deep greens of Oregon—forests, hills, and farmland. Pubah saw that the rivers ran through the forests, the forests surrounded the farms, the hills graduated to mountains and the great snowcapped mountains touched the sky.

Pubah relaxed and put her arms around Lazy and looked down at the living, breathing, peopled earth from which, for some moments in time through some magnificent grace, they were released into a distance great enough to allow them to look upon the mother that held them all. She suddenly let go of her panic to rush around and fix everything.

"Lazy, do you think I should stop rushing around, trying to save the world? It looks pretty safe to me."

Lazy smiled. "Yes, the world looks safe."

"I'd like to travel," Pubah said. "I'd like to go to Europe, to Italy . . ."

Suddenly Lazy looked out into the clouds as though she saw something there. "What is it?" Pubah wanted to know. "What do you see?"

"Something about what you're saying," Lazy muttered, "something from a dream . . . . You *will* travel." She squinted into the distance and tried to remember the dream she had on the balloon as it drifted over the ocean, the important dream about mountains and a volcanic eruption. The forgotten dream reappeared before her. "I see mountains," she told Pubah. "Do you see them? Mountains and a volcano?"

Pubah said, "I think St. Helens is in the other direction, Lazy. Over there . . ." She began to turn, but Lazy wouldn't let her.

"No, not that volcano. Another one. Can't you see it?"

Pubah looked at Lazy who appeared rather distant and mystic, the way she looked sometimes when she was writing. She tried to see what Lazy was seeing. She listened to her words with such intensity that Lazy's vision began to form before her.

"A volcano," Lazy continued, "that erupted thousands of years ago. Do you see it?"

Pubah nodded. She saw it. A fragment of the dream Lazy had dreamed when she was lost in the balloon now appeared before them in such vivid color they could almost reach out and touch it.

122

There was Pubah, some years hence, leading an excavation to a lavish but crumbling villa in Italy, a villa that for centuries had been buried under volcanic rock.

"That's you, Pubah, leading an excavation to the Villa dei Papiri near Naples."

Lazy's voice gave Pubah a chill. With a wave of her hand, Lazy made the dream continue. "Sealed off by a volcanic eruption for thousands of years, the Villa is known to be a treasure house of ancient documents. Look! Carson has discovered an entrance."

They saw the old whippet stepping daintily across the rocks, sniffing out a secret doorway.

"That entrance has been lost to anthropologists and historians for centuries," Lazy went on, "and you and Carson find it! There you are, bent over, carrying one of your solar lanterns into a dark tunnel and then you see a vault, filled with scrolls."

"I think I read about that volcano in *National Geographic*," Pubah whispered.

"Shh, watch. You're picking up one of the scrolls but, oh dear, it turns to dust in your hands. It's become carbonized in the tomb; but wait, see how useful your inventiveness is."

They watched as Pubah reached into her pack and pulled out some chemicals. In a moment, on the spot, she invented an enzyme that allowed her to unfurl the scrolls without damage, then begin to transcribe the scrolls by the light of the lantern.

"What do they say?" Pubah wanted to know as she watched her vision. "I can't see what they say from here."

Lazy blinked and waved her hand like a wand across the sky. "The next part of the dream looks like this. There you are, see? At the Congress of Papyrology giving a report on your texts, revealing the truth found in those scrolls."

secret doorway

"I'm reading from them to those people." Pubah watched herself reading to the great convention.

Lazy nodded her head. "You're reporting on an old document. You're trying to get something across to them and they're getting it. I can't quite see . . . oh yes, now I get it. Your report is on a document that was trying to straighten something out, something that had been confused for thousands of years before the document was ever written, but the volcano had buried it before the world could hear what it had to say. It was . . ." Lazy concentrated and the image materialized, ". . . it was a report that meant to clarify once and for all some ancient words that had been misunderstood for millenia."

"What is it? What's in that old report?"

"Listen."

They listened and heard Pubah's voice, off in the future, reading to the papyrologists. She was quoting a recovered letter, she said, to Tacitus from the younger Plina. She read:

> Dearest Tacitus,
>
> Thank you for directing me to Queen Nea's library here in Egypt. I have found fascinating writings of great importance. Some evenings I am here long after the others have gone off to bed.
>
> One item of note, especially in light of our conversation last summer on how language can either confine or free us—I found some ancient texts discussing the true meanings of words we moderns have misunderstood. One such text explains the etymology of "marriage" and "to marry," for example, and states that it does not come from *tumaritus* (meaning to set off two by two), as we have long thought. No. The actual root is *unmarias* or *unomaritarias* or *unomarianias*—in Greek *unmeirax*, which all mean *to make a blessed union of opposites within one's self, an inner communion, so to speak, of the inner male and female who then give birth to—and set free—the divine and immortal child, the inner Self* . . . The text says all human beings are meant to marry like this.
>
> The pages are crumbling, Tacitus, and nearly lost, but I can still make out one thing that must be saved at all costs: Those who are married in this way are found to be childlike and inclined to celebrate life. No doubt you've met some of them, just as I have, and didn't even know what they were. From now on I intend to keep an eye out for the happy ones, my friend. They are the ones truly married.
>
> In hopes that your own inner Self may break free in this serious world . . . .
>
> Your Loving Friend,
> Plina the Librarian, Currently of Egypt

Lazy raised her binoculars. "I think all those italics are Plina's," she said.

"Your visions are so detailed, Laze," Pubah commended her.

"Thank you," Lazy was rather proud of herself. "They have to be. I'm a writer. But back to the dream. Yes, there you are, continuing to speak. Talking about how sad it was that volcanic eruptions had buried this message for almost too long until your discovery—and Carson's—of the secret entrance. And look!" They watched as the crowd of papyrologists stood up and cheered.

"Well, I guess we're the marrying kind after all," Lazy marveled, putting her binoculars down.

"I guess we are," Pubah smiled, "But, Lazy . . ."

"Yes?" They put their arms around each other.

"If what Plina said is true and everybody knows it, then thirty or fifty years from now we'll look back and see that what saved the world wasn't anything we invented or wrote."

"No?" Lazy blinked, catching a few moments of another dream about Pubah and writing and inventions. "What will have saved the world then?"

"Just how we live our lives. That's all. That's it."

"You're a very wise woman, Pubah."

"I am kind of, aren't I?"

"Yep."

Pubah squeezed Lazy and then marched around the balloon's basket, stomping her feet and congratulating herself. There was nothing that made her quite so happy as to have Lazy think she was wise.

"I am, actually, very wise. I've noticed it myself. I'm a wise one, all right."

Lazy warned her. "You'd better watch all that stomping, Pubah." She pointed down to the river below them. "You know if you fall through the bottom of this basket, you'll land right in the river and . . ." she shook her head slowly, "you just never know what might be in the water."

Pubah stopped stomping. "I hate things that might be in the water! I hate things that might be in the water!"

Lazy tossed her head back and laughed and laughed until soon Pubah and all the birds in the sky and all the fish in the rivers and all the creatures on earth joined in, and the universe heard this laughing, and was touched by it, and fell forever into love.

The End

Andrea Carlisle was born and raised in North Dakota, studied at the University of Iowa Writers' Workshop where she received a degree in English and Creative Writing, and now lives in Portland, Oregon. She has worked as a counselor and consultant for adolescent programs, as a writing instructor, and as a writer for various state and local businesses and bureaucracies. Her fiction has appeared in CALYX, *A Journal of Art and Literature by Women, Willow Springs,* and *Northwest Review.* For her creative writing, she has earned an Oregon Arts Commission Individual Artists Fellowship, a citation as an "outstanding writer" by the Pushcart Awards, and selection as a participant in the Bread Loaf Writers' Conference in Vermont. In 1985-86 she co-authored, co-produced, and co-directed a 30 minute video program called "Looking Up." The video won a first place award at the John Muir Medical Film Festival, honorable mention at the San Francisco International Film Festival, and was a finalist in the American Film Festival. She lives on a houseboat on the Multnomah Channel of the Columbia River where she continues to write.

The text of this
book is composed in Goudy.
Typeset by the Production Department,
Eugene, Oregon.